FIND MY SISTER

When private investigator Al Maclean rescues Gail Grant from being assaulted in her hotel room, he has no inkling that she will become his next client. Gail is searching for her sister, who mysteriously disappeared from her hotel room two years ago, and Maclean's brief is simple: *Find my sister!* But his task is far from easy, as it turns out to involve criminal menace and murder . . . And in *Arrest Ace Lannigan!*, the star reporter of a London paper is out to bust a ring of American hoodlums terrorising the country.

NORMAN FIRTH

FIND MY SISTER

Complete and Unabridged

LINFORD
Leicester

First published in Great Britain

First Linford Edition
published 2017

A catalogue record for this book is available
from the British Library.

ISBN 978–1–4448–3454–3

Published by
F. A. Thorpe (Publishing)
Anstey, Leicestershire

Set by Words & Graphics Ltd.
Anstey, Leicestershire
Printed and bound in Great Britain by
T. J. International Ltd., Padstow, Cornwall

This book is printed on acid-free paper

Find My Sister

1

You Can't Lick Maclean

Al Maclean relaxed his six-foot-odd of muscle and brawn on the well-worn but comfortable settee, and grinned. You couldn't lick Maclean — nobody could!

The cops thought they had when they'd taken away his licence to act as a private detective. They hadn't liked his methods. But Maclean didn't worry any about that. He was well known — he got results — and people who wanted a first-rate dick would still seek him out; he knew that. And if the cops wouldn't give him a licence again, okay, he'd work without one, and to hell with the whole blasted department of the N.Y. Gendarmerie.

He drew on his smoke, trickled the fumes through his nostrils, and gave the room he was in a second look-over. It was okay. He decided he'd made no mistake in coming here. Here the cops wouldn't think of looking for him — if they ever wanted him that badly. He'd been sorry to close up his downtown office, but what the hell? This was just as good — he felt right at home here in the Rose Graham Hotel.

The Rose Graham huddled its thirteen floors between its two neighbouring forty-floor buildings. It looked small and tawdry up against those two, but it didn't show any sign of insignificance itself. It looked, from the facade, haughtily old-fashioned. Which it was. Outside it looked like a hotel of the '20s. Inside it looked the same way. But it was comfortable, and it was no more than a stone's throw from Times Square. No, you wouldn't expect to find a joint like this so near to a vital pulse of the city; but here it was, and here it was going to remain — as long as Rose Graham had her way. And since Rose Graham was a very determined woman, it was likely to stick around for a long time, and then some.

Rose Graham had come over to America from England some twenty-two years before. She had come to star in the Broadway production of the English success, *Wild Gander*. Maybe you remember what a colossal flop that play was. It ran four nights, then folded up rapidly, and the backer and producer slid out of town and hightailed it for parts unknown, leaving the cast high and dry.

One of the cast was Rose Graham, and not having the money to get back to England, she had married a rich old sugar-daddy who'd been haunting her ever since she'd arrived. She'd picked well; for the bald eighty-year-old oil king was so doddery he couldn't even do anything about the fact that Rose didn't know what love meant — she being only seventeen in those days. Furthermore, in his desire to prove himself a better husband than he was, he started tossing down patent remedies for regaining lost youth and submitting to glandular operations in the hope he'd come out of them looking and feeling like Rudolph Valentino. It was while under one of these that his heart called it a day and ceased to beat. Nor could half a dozen specialists wind it up for him again.

So Rose Latour — now the Widow Graham — inherited all his money and estate, along with which was a small hotel quite near to Times Square, which the old man had scheduled for demolition, meaning to build a super saloon there. There was a long-term lease on the place; and although plenty of folks thought the hotel was an eyesore that should be removed to make way for something more fitting to the style of the great city, they hadn't been able to do anything about it, not even when Rose had turned it into a guest house for 'resting' vaudeville artists. Yes, that was Rose — a heart as big as her two now-pendulous bosoms.

She didn't charge the hard-up actors a cent. Any theatre folk down on their luck were welcome if there was room. Rose lived there herself, acting as kind of mother, as well as father-confessor, to all sorts and descriptions of characters.

That was one side of her. The other side, though, was apt to obscure the side just described. For with the old boy's money she had set Broadway aflame, producing and acting in lavish musical spectacles, until she got past it. All the time she toted round a whole string of gigolos and hangers-on. She threw her money about; but no matter how fast she threw it, it wouldn't ever come to an end — her late husband had been several times several a millionaire.

She lived gloriously and freely, and enjoyed every second of her colourful life. She wouldn't have had it any other way; and if, when she grew older, and wrinkles crept round her blue eyes, and the rouge looked hectically red on her lined, taut cheeks; if other women said she had to *pay* her escorts — well, she didn't care about that either. Just so long as she kept living. She was like a precious stone — one side rough and uncut; the other cut and polished into a million gaudy facets that sparkled and winked in the neon world of Broadway.

And every day, broken-down old actors found refuge at her hotel. That was why Maclean was there; he wasn't any actor, but he was broken-down, at least as far as money was concerned. He knew Rose

Graham — 'Good-time Rosie', as they called her — well; in fact, everybody who was nobody in New York knew her. And when she had heard what the cops had done to his licence, she said: 'Sure, it's a shame, Al. Suppose you come over to my hotel — give you the best room!' Which suited Al Maclean, since he lived from case to food — in other words, spent every cent he earned as he earned it.

There he was, then. It was old-fashioned, but it was cosy. He felt at home already. He had a top-floor room — a 'penthouse apartment', as Rose had humorously informed him. He'd been moved in about two hours, and he'd just finished unpacking.

He stubbed out his cigarette in the nearby tray — then listened keenly as his ears caught a sound from the next room. It had seemed like a woman's scream! It had been cut off abruptly; Maclean waited tensely. He heard a chair clatter over, then a scuffling noise, and another quickly stilled shriek.

With Maclean, instinct thought for him; in one jump he was at the door and into the passage. He skidded along to the next door and listened. Yes — there was another clatter as something went over. He tried the door handle. It was locked. From inside issued a muffled sobbing.

Maclean shot back to his room, then returned carrying a set of master keys. He began to try them. The third one fitted; he twisted it and entered the room. 'Some party,' he grated as he took in details. 'Can anyone join in?'

It was, as Maclean had said, 'some party'! There was a middle-aged, thin-featured, sadistic-looking man dressed in a smoking jacket and pyjamas. He was bending over a young woman; Maclean reckoned her age at roughly about seventeen. Her flimsy summer frock had been ripped and torn and was hanging in shreds from her left arm. Her ash-blonde hair was disheveled, and her light make-up smeared with tears. She was sobbing hysterically, and had apparently been fighting off the man. She saw Maclean and eluded the momentarily spellbound man by jumping away from him and rushing to Maclean's side.

Maclean slipped an arm about her shoulders and said: 'Take it easy, honey. What's happened?'

'Oh, please — please take me away. I — I can't stay here with him any longer. I — '

'You don't have to, baby. How come you're here in the first place?'

The thin man's face was crimping into an ugly scowl. He grunted: 'Get out of here, whoever you are, or by God — '

'Sit down, brother,' growled Maclean.

The thin fellow's veins stood out like ridges on his forehead. His hand slid into the pocket of his smoking jacket.

'Oh, look out!' shrilled the woman. 'His — his knife — '

The thin man's hand was in view again. So was a long throwing knife, lodged precariously in the palm of his hand.

Which was what Maclean had waited for: the excuse to lamp this mug long and hard. The knife-man hardly saw Maclean move at all; before he knew what the blur was, Maclean's balled fist cannoned into his jawbone, and he literally rose into the air and spun towards the fireplace,

10

landing with his head against the fender. Maclean, tough as ever, went right after him, and kicked his knife hand until blood gushed from his crushed fingers, and the knife slid limply to the floor. The man jerked and heaved in agony, breath whistling through his teeth in harsh rasps.

Maclean said: 'I may want you later, brother.'

He went back to the shivering woman, moved her gently into the passage, and locked the door behind them, taking the key from the inside. He took her to his own room and gave her his overcoat to wrap round her. 'So what's all this all about?' he finally asked.

The woman sipped the brandy he'd given her and coughed a little. She turned big blue eyes upon Maclean, and his heart fluttered a little.

Maclean had only ever loved one woman — a Eurasian called Lala Cortini. To him she had been everything he ever wanted in a woman. His sanity had deserted him for a time when she had died — for him — in tragic circumstances. But he could always see what was exquisite in the way of women. This kid before him was, and he didn't wonder she'd run into trouble with looks like hers, and a soft, rounded figure like she had.

She began to tell him her story. 'My name is Gail Grant. I want — I want to thank you. I don't know what Salato would have done to me if you hadn't arrived.'

'I do,' said Maclean grimly. 'But skip that. How come you got in a locked room with him, and who is he?'

'He's a vaudeville act. I was his assistant. You know the kind of act — I stand against a board while he throws knives all around me.'

'Sure, I know. Corny these days, isn't it?'

'I'm afraid it is. That's why we couldn't get any work, I expect.'

'You don't seem to be the type of gal to be hooked up with show business,' Maclean told her. 'You seem more like you should be going to some hick high school.'

'I was, until about three months ago. I

was in a small town called Rushville in the Midwest. But I wanted to come to New York, and when my — my father died, I had enough money to do so.'

'And you were going to take your chances in a place like New York all alone?'

She shook her head and sipped more brandy. While she had been talking the coat had slipped open, and Maclean had to admire her smooth knees with their delicate pink shading. She went on: 'I hadn't planned on being alone. I expected to find my elder sister here, you see. But things went wrong. She wasn't here when I arrived, and the room she occupied was now occupied by Salato. It seems she left almost two years ago without telling anyone where she was going.'

'Two years? Hell! But how about the letters you had from her? How about those?'

'I hadn't had any for two years. You see, she ran away from home against Dad's wishes when she was twenty. She wrote me secretly from this hotel, and I used to write back. Then the letters stopped coming, and none of mine were ever answered after that. They were all returned unopened.'

'Then you might have guessed she wasn't here anymore!'

'I did; but I thought they might know where she'd gone. They don't. Anyway, after I'd paid the fare here, I didn't have a whole lot of money left, and I knew I'd have to get a job while I searched for her. But I couldn't. Miss Graham here said I could have a room free until I found my feet; that helped. Then, two months ago, Salato called me to his room and said he had heard I wanted a job. He told me that if his act had a pretty woman in it, he was sure to get work. It sounded wonderful, the idea of going on the stage, and he was awfully polite and kind to me. We rehearsed the knife routine, and I soon got used to it. But we never did get a steady job; just one-night stands at floor shows and that kind of thing.'

'I see. That was two months ago?'

'Yes. I didn't get much, but I did get enough to see me through. Salato was quite a gentleman at first, but then he began to maul me, and once he suggested something lewd. I said if he didn't stop, I'd leave the act right there and then, and he apologised. Well, today he called me to his room — said he had a new costume for me for the act, and would I try it on for size. He said I could change behind the screen in his room, but just when . . . well, halfway through changing my dress he came over and told me I was a teasing little vixen, then attacked me.'

'I get it. Hmm! Intend to report him?'

'No. No, I won't do that. It wouldn't be very nice publicity for the hotel, and Miss Graham has been so kind.'

'I've been thinking,' said Maclean. 'You certainly need this big sister of yours. Maybe *I* can find her!'

2

Maclean Takes a Hand

Gail knew Maclean for an ally right away. She liked the burly honesty of him, the keen stare of his eyes, the strong set of his jaw. She told him all she could about her sister, which wasn't very much. When she had finished, Maclean saw her to her room, said he'd meet her at seven for dinner, and went downstairs to find Rose Graham.

'Good-time Rosie' was at home. She was in her lower-floor apartments, reclining on a low divan, a cloud of scented cigarette smoke swirling round her heavily rouged cheeks. As Maclean knocked and entered, she gazed up languidly.

'Oh, hello, Al. How's things?'

'They're all right with me,' he told her. 'But you don't look so bright.'

She admitted she didn't feel so bright. 'Look, Al — how do you ever manage to keep as spry as you are? Your life's been a pretty hard one, hey? Well, my life ain't been exactly rosy, but look at me! Look at these derned bags under my eyes! They're so big a porter'd charge double for carryin' them!'

Maclean grinned and said, 'You want to keep off the late nights, Good Time. You can't stay up half the night doing this and that, and expect to stay young and keep that schoolgirl complexion.'

'Hmm. Maybe you're right at that. But — what the hell! What's the sense in me wantin' to look young an' all that? Why, even if I had the face of Shirley Temple, I'd still have this oversized bust.'

Maclean grinned. 'That doesn't count, Rosie. It's the big heart that beats underneath.'

'Sure, sure — but guys don't look at the big heart. Tell me, Al — you think I've lost my appeal?'

'Sure, Rosie,' he told her frankly. 'You lost that years ago. All you got now is personality.'

Good Time Rosie sighed and relaxed back on the cushions. She patted the divan by her knees, and Al went over and sat there. He said: 'I just came to tell you, Rosie, that you've got a skunk on the top floor who attacks young women.'

'*What?*' Rosie sat up suddenly. 'What d'you mean, Al? Who is it?'

'A louse called Salato.'

'Salato? Hell! I never did like the set of that mug. What's he done now?'

'Nothing much — or a whole lot, according to your point of view. He tried to criminally assault his female assistant, that's all.'

Rosie's lips set grimly. 'Oh *that's* all, is it? Well I can tell you *my* point of view on that kinda thing, Al. Out he goes right now. I hate them skunks who attack young women.'

'I knew you'd see it that way, Rosie. I locked him in his room — I'll let him know you said to scram when I get back again. There's something else I wanted to ask you while I'm here. This woman, the one he attacked — Gail Grant, her name is — '

'Yeah, sure. She's a sweet kid, Al. I'm sorry the big lug did that to her. But it seems you managed to step in just in time. An' her just come from the country, more or less, looking for her sister. Poor kid!'

'That's what I wanted to talk about,' Al told her. 'That sister of hers — Melanie Grant. The kid says she stayed here for some time. That so?'

'Sure, Al, that's so. She stayed here a year or so. Roomed at the top with another lady.'

'And when she left, she didn't leave any forwarding address?'

'She didn't exactly leave, Al. Leastways, not officially. She useta work at the Golden Garter Club on 42nd, together with the woman she roomed with, a Maisie Grey. Maisie hooked some rich socialite and married the guy — Frederick F. Fredericks, his name was.'

'What does the middle F stand for — Frederick?' grinned Maclean.

'Farnum, I think. Anyway, soon after Maisie married this bird, Melanie Grant started out for the club one night and never came back. I phoned the club a coupla days later and found out she never even got there that night. She simply vanished from the face of New York between here an' 42nd Street. Nobody's ever seen or heard of her since, to my knowledge. Course, I reported the matter to the bulls, but what's one missing woman amongst thousands? I reckon they thought she'd slung herself in the river, or run off with some rich old sucker, or gotten herself murdered down in China-town or something. That's how it goes.'

'And is that what you think?'

'Nope, that ain't what I think, Al. If she run off with a married man, why did she leave her luggage? She left some dainty dresses an' a whole lot of jewellery behind. If she jumped in the river, I don't see why. She hadn't no worries at all; she was always cheerful. Earned lotsa dough at that Golden Garter joint.'

'But suppose she got herself bumped off?'

'That could be the answer, but can you see anyone getting rubbed out between here and 42nd? Why, it's a straight run through the busiest part of the city.'

Maclean said: 'Well, maybe we'll find

out. That kid upstairs needs her, an' I'm putting myself on the case. How about letting me take a gander through her stuff, Rosie?'

'Sure; I was meaning to hand it over to her sister, but it slipped my mind. You can take a look through it first of all.' She got up with considerable puffing, hoisted the filmy dressing robe she was wearing jauntily with one hand, and crossed to a nearby cupboard. From this she took three large cases, brought them over and set them on the table. 'There they are, Al. That was her whole wardrobe.'

They were unlocked. Maclean thought that was funny, too. If Melanie Grant had known she wasn't coming back again, would she have left her stuff open for anyone to help themselves to? Wouldn't she have left a note for it to be sent to her family, to her younger sister? It was certainly worth having. The three evening gowns were delightful, although now out of fashion. The dainty shoes and evening slippers must have cost plenty. The street clothes were tailored, well-cut, by a notable firm. There were flimsy underclothes, still faintly perfumed.

He said: 'What did this woman look like, Rosie?'

Rose smiled and thought back. 'One of the finest — she had to be to get a job at the Golden Garter. Golden hair, red lips, smooth refined features, mysterious eyes. Her figure was calculated to make Hedy Lemarr green with envy, and she didn't mind showing it if she felt the occasion warranted it. She used to do an act with two other women at the club. But nobody watched the others — they couldn't take their eyes offa Melanie, who was the centre one.'

Maclean was still searching the cases, but he failed to find anything apart from the clothing and shoes. Finally he said: 'Okay, Good Time, I'll take these along to the little lady, and tell Salato to blow before I throw him out on his ear.'

'You do that, Al. I don't want no dirty scheming roués in my hotel. It's respectable! Can you imagine the nerve of the guy!'

Maclean returned upstairs, leaving the indignant woman still cursing Salato and all his works. He went to Salato's room door, opened it, and walked in. The man had vanished, and Maclean noted the open window leading to the fire escape. There was a scrap of paper on the table, which Maclean picked up. It read: 'I'll remember you, my friend. I don't forget a face. You'll be sorry you ever interfered with me — no one can stomp on my knife-hand and get away with it. As soon as the wounds heal, look out for yourself.'

Maclean grinned, screwed the note up, crossed to the window, and looked down. Far below, in the side alley, a thin figure was hastening away. Maclean yelled: 'Hey!'

The figure stopped, and the face of Salato, convulsed with rage, peered up. He shook his fist at the grinning detective. Maclean made a rude gesture, tossed the crumpled note down into the alley, and, losing interest, returned to his own room.

He lazed around then, until seven. At five to seven precisely, he picked Gail Grant up from her room. She had donned one of her sister's gowns, which Maclean had given her earlier, and in it she looked ravishing, although slightly nervous. Maclean admired her openly, and she quavered: 'Al' — she called him that now — 'Do I look all right?'

'Honey, if we meet any Hollywood talent scouts, you'll be starring in movies inside a week.'

'Oh, don't kid me,' she told him. 'I — I feel naked. Well, practically naked.'

'You are — practically,' he agreed. 'But so what? You won't be the only one, and what would you want to do with a figure like yours if you didn't show it?'

She blushed, but was flattered by his words.

Maclean took her along to Romany's and watched her eagerness as she ordered, and gazed about interestedly at the hundreds of fashionable diners. He himself hardly ate; he watched Gail's animated face — the intrigued delight she took in being in a fashionable night spot, dining with a well-dressed man of the world. Colour came richly to her cheeks as she sipped champagne, and her eyes sparkled.

'This is wonderful, Al,' she told him. 'Thank you ever so much for bringing me.'

'Think nothing of it. Get a load of the floor show — it's just starting now.'

He detected traces of shocked shame in her eyes as she watched the languorous dark-eyed woman who held the floor, divesting herself of her already scant clothing to musical accompaniment. 'Oh, how could any woman expose her body to — to — well, like that! It's horrible!'

'You're not a prude, kid, are you?' asked Maclean quietly.

'Me? Why, no — I don't think so. I mean, if you're in love with someone . . . ' She gazed meaningfully at Maclean, then flushed and continued hurriedly. 'Well, then it's — it's different.'

Maclean grinned. 'You must learn not to be so naïve, kid. Act as if you were part of New York, not as if you were fresh up from the milk pails and the new-mown hay, or whatever they have in the burg you come from. You have to be wide to get by in the city. Maybe if you hadn't seemed so innocent, Salato would have left you alone.'

She shook her head. 'I couldn't pretend to be something I'm not. I'd hate to be like — well, like *her*, for instance.' She pointed discreetly to a young woman nearby.

Maclean followed her direction and took the woman in. Over the back of her chair was an expensive sable wrap. The woman herself was wearing a white gown studded with brilliants that revealed her figure brazenly, as if she had been wearing nothing at all. It fitted like elastic, sneaking tightly in and out of every curve. Her face was full of paint and powder; Maclean thought maybe she had her own special cosmetic factory working for her. He began to see why there'd been a shortage of powder and lipstick lately — this lady had it all on her face! But underneath the paint was a trace of beauty and grace. When the woman moved, she moved charmingly, as if she had had long and hard lessons in deportment. Maclean thought that maybe she had once been a model.

Then he heard her name above the incessant chatter around. She was speaking to the man to her left, and he said: 'I trust your husband is a little better this evening, Mrs. Fredericks? Sorry to hear he's been confined to bed. Dashed unpleasant for a busy fellow like him.'

'Oh yes,' she replied, smiling. 'Freddie's much better, thank you. He works too hard, that's the trouble. He isn't as young as he used to be,' she said with a hint of scorn in her voice.

But Maclean wasn't listening anymore. The woman was a Mrs. Fredericks, and her husband's name seemed to be Freddie — Freddie Fredericks, and she was young and he was old! And, obviously, she had deportment — which she would naturally have had if she had been a show woman. It was too big to be coincidence — the woman seated so near them was obviously Melanie Grant's one-time roommate who had married rich!

The strip-artist had finished her act now. Maclean called a waiter and scribbled on a piece of paper: 'I must see you — important', then gave it to the waiter to take to Mrs. Fredericks. She opened it with a murmured apology to her table. Then she looked questioningly at the waiter, who nodded towards

Maclean. She sent a message back, scribbled on the back of a visiting card: 'In the foyer here — eleven-thirty.'

3

Maisie Makes a Play

Maclean took Gail home early. His unexpected encounter with the woman who had once, and not long ago, been Melanie Grant's roommate had caused him to change his plans. The urge to get right into the case there and then was on him.

Gail didn't argue, and Maclean saw her safely back to the Rose Graham. Then, because he still had time to spare before he was due to meet the interesting Mrs. Fredericks, he took the cab round to the Golden Garter Club, where once Melanie Grant had done her strip act.

He didn't have any trouble getting in; since the repeal of Prohibition, the Golden Garter had been open for all comers. Their big attraction, now that illicit liquor was a bygone, was a risqué floor show. Perhaps risqué doesn't do the show justice — perhaps the better word would be 'blue', in the nastiest sense of the word. But Maclean wasn't there to see floor shows of any kind; he was there for information. He tried the staff entrance, and got talking to the door-keeper there.

'Know a Melanie Grant?' Maclean asked.

'Why sure. Who doesn't! That kid was dynamite. Maybe if she'd kept in the night-club business, she'd have gotten to where Texas Guinan once got. But she didn't.'

'I know she didn't. That's what I want to ask you about. If you can help me trace her, there's twenty bucks for you.'

The doorkeeper shook his head regretfully. 'Guess not, mister. You see, it seems she just vanished without leaving a word she was going. She had some clothing down here at the club — she didn't even pick that up. Even the two women who used to do her dance with her didn't know where she'd blown to. Sorry I can't help. I could have used the dollars.'

'Maybe you can still have them,'

Maclean told him. 'Think back. The woman must have had some boyfriends if she was as come-hither as people reckon. How about that?'

'Oh sure, she toted around the usual sugar-daddies, stage-door johnnies and city wolves, but I don't recollect her going more than twice with any one of 'em . . . though yeah, that's right! She did have one guy who called pretty regular for her. Lemme see . . . he was some big shot; used to give me his card to take to her dressing room with flowers. What was it . . . ? Forster? No. Folkestone? Nope. Forester — that's it! Michael Forester, the hotel owner. Maybe you know him — he owns about half the better-class dumps in town.'

'Sure, I know him. And you say she seemed pretty stuck on this guy?'

'I didn't say on the guy himself. If you ask me, his dough had something to do with it. What would a cutie like Melanie be doin' with a bald-headed old runt if he didn't have dough?'

'You tell me,' suggested Maclean. 'I guess you've got the right angle on it at that. Anything else you can tell me? How about the two dames who used to dance with her?'

'Nope — they were as surprised as anyone else. The only one who might tell you anything more was the gal she used to room with, who got herself hitched just before Melanie vanished.'

'Maisie Grey — now Mrs. Frederick F. Fredericks?'

'You know her?'

'I will before very long. That's all you know?'

'So help me it is. If you third-degreed me, I couldn't speak another line on the subject.'

Maclean gave him the twenty dollars. He hadn't that much to spare really, but he was that kind of a guy — he threw what he had to the wind, and usually it came back in the teeth of a gale. That was what would have to happen this time. He didn't worry about giving away hunks of his unsubstantial bankroll. He was casting bread on the waters, and he relied on it to come back buttered. It generally did. On both sides!

He took a glance at his wristwatch, nodded, picked up a cab again, and gave the destination. He was waiting at the appointed spot for five minutes before Maisie Fredericks arrived. She came furtively almost, with two or three sideways and backwards glances. As her eyes fell on him, they lit up with sudden interest, and she hurried towards him.

'Maclean is my name. I believe yours is Mrs. Frederick F. Fredericks?'

'Why yes, I am Mrs. Fredericks. I was rather surprised to get your note. I don't believe I know you, do I?'

Her eyes ran up and down his burly figure, his square-cut face, and the neat fit of his suit. She took in the breadth of his shoulders, and her eyes kindled. Maclean looked in those eyes and hated what he saw there. He had often seen men eyeing women with that same expression.

'Your note intrigued me, I must confess. I'm not in the habit of making assignations this way, Mr. Maclean; but you're rather an interesting person, aren't you?'

'Am I?' said Maclean, without any

alteration in his tone. 'Maybe. I don't actually have any designs on you, Mrs. Fredericks.'

She laughed silkily. 'Haven't you? What a dreadful pity! Still, perhaps that difficulty can be overcome. You must have heard about me?'

'I haven't heard anything particularly. I simply noticed you in the club when your name was spoken. I would have looked for you sooner or later, though — there's something I need to discuss with you.'

'Here and now?'

'This is as good a place as any. The time is immaterial.'

She shook her head. 'I'm very disappointed in you, Mr. Maclean. I anticipated something a little more exciting than a flat discussion in public. And if that's all you require, I'm afraid I can't accommodate you. So sorry.'

'This may be exciting enough.'

'Oh come, Mr. Maclean. I'll strike a bargain with you. You rather interest me.'

'Thanks,' Maclean said dryly.

'And when anyone interests me, I like to get to know them better. If you'll come home with me and have a cocktail, I'll listen to what you have to say there. Will you?'

'Your husband — '

'Is confined to his bed after a nervous breakdown.'

'The servants?'

'Are quite used to my little ways with regards to gentlemen friends. What is more, my husband trusts me — poor fool!'

Maclean smiled. He couldn't help it. Certainly this woman was straightforward with herself and her would-be conquests. 'I'll come. But I'm in no mood for scenes. Get me?'

'I think so, and I assure you my husband is not yet able to leave his bed. He will not surprise us.'

'Are you always this free with your invitations?' asked Maclean as they left the hotel.

'Generally.' She piloted him to a car that was parked on the lot next to the Romany. 'My car, Mr. Maclean — oh, what's your first name?'

'Al.'

'It doesn't suit you — Al always makes me think of a weak sort of man. I thought you'd have had a name like Grant or Clark or maybe Robert.'

'I like it,' Maclean told her. Then they were in the car, and she said nothing further until they had turned into the driveway of a big Westchester mansion. She dismissed the chauffeur and guided Maclean round to a small door at the rear of the place.

'I always keep this entrance for my . . . friends,' she explained. 'It will be just as well to be as silent as possible.'

Maclean had to admire her nerve. To carry out her intrigues under the very roof of the house her husband inhabited was the essence of nerve — or wantonness! Or maybe both. But, he reflected grimly, she was due for a slight shock in his case.

It was quiet in the mansion. She took his hand, and in spite of himself, electric shivers chased up his backbone, setting his mind on fire with her presence. He took the stairs quietly at her side, and as they passed a room at the top of the staircase she inclined her head towards it and stated: 'He's in there — Rip Van Winkle himself. I must go and say good night to him — please excuse me. If you'll go in the third room on the right, I'll join you immediately.'

Maclean followed her directions. The door opened easily, and he went in. It was a large room, decorated throughout in murals of doubtful taste. It was the kind of room he would have expected of this woman, but nevertheless he was surprised to find that her husband permitted it. His lip curled as he thought of that. Fredericks must be a weak fool! He found a decanter of rye, poured himself a glass, and threw it down his throat. It warmed him.

Maisie came in then, and shook her head as he opened his mouth to speak. Before he could frame a sentence, she had passed into an adjoining chamber and closed the door. He waited impatiently. It all seemed so fantastic, so impossible — no, not impossible; improbable! Yet it was happening, and to him! He had heard of women like this, but he hadn't ever expected to meet one. They were too rare.

There came the soft turn of a door handle, and he spun round and looked at her as she stood facing him in the doorway. She had taken off her revealing gown and replaced it with an even more revealing nightgown and negligee. He said shortly: 'I suppose you do this kind of thing for excitement?'

Her eyes became angry. She snapped: 'What other excitement can a woman get, if she's married to a damned useless old fool?'

'That's neither here nor there. If I was your husband, I'd shoot you — or myself! Or both! But I'm one sucker you won't make a conquest of. So don't try any more acts.'

'So why did you send that note?' she snarled. 'Why did you come here? Do you think I didn't know it was all an act to get to know me? Well, now you *do*, and you aren't satisfied!'

'You're wrong. I came here because I wanted to ask you some questions. I still do, and I'm going to.'

'Who — who *are* you then? *What* are you?'

'I'm Maclean, all right — I wasn't kidding there. I'm a private detective, and that's why I'm here.'

'A detective?' she sneered. 'Hmm! What do you want to know?'

'Only one thing — where is Melanie Grant?'

4

Maisie Isn't Talking

Maclean was astonished at the change those simple words inspired. He had thought nothing would shock Maisie out of her blasé self-control; thought he could have said anything, done anything, without causing her to do more than raise an eyebrow. But that one sentence rocked her as a physical blow would have done. Her face drew taut and hard, her body stiffened, and she stared at him without attempting to speak. Beneath the mask of rouge and powder lurked the first faint dawning of fear — surprised fear!

Maclean said: 'You didn't expect that?'

Still she didn't answer him. Her hand clenched by her side as she struggled for control and gained it. Her features dropped into the expressionless, gaudy mask they had been before. Her tense body relaxed, and she lay back on the bed, staring up at him.

'You *do* know something,' said Maclean grimly.

She selected a cigarette from a handy box and lit it. She blew smoke thoughtfully in his face and said: 'Am I supposed to?'

'You are. You once roomed with her, didn't you? That's what I wanted to discuss with you, lady. Just what do you know?'

'Very little — I've no objection to telling you. She was a fine woman and a clever artiste. We roomed for a couple of years. I wasn't ever really close to her — I doubt if anyone was. Then I got married, and the last I heard of her she had . . . vanished.'

'Are you trying to tell me you didn't see her at all after you were married?'

'Why should I? I've told you we weren't really intimate friends. It was convenient to share our rooms, and we did. That's all. We both went to the Rose Graham Hotel when we were out of work — it was a bad year for vaudeville, and 'Good Time' Rosie only had the one room left. She said we could share it, and we did.

41

We kept to that arrangement even after we'd gotten work at the Golden Garter.'

'You've no idea where Melanie Grant went? Or — what might have happened to her?'

'None.'

'Remember her having any boyfriends — any particular ones?'

'Melanie had no boyfriends apart from a few hangers-on that all showgirls accumulate.'

'You're sure of that?'

'Certain!'

'Then how about Michael Forester?' snapped Maclean.

Only her eyes flickered; her face was expressionless still. 'Forester?' she said vaguely.

'The same — Forester the hotel owner. Wasn't he one of her 'steadies'?'

'I really couldn't say. I can't remember having heard of him before.'

'Can't you? Now that's rather strange. He was so attached to Melanie Grant that even the doorman at the club noticed his comings and goings. It's kind of funny that you missed him yourself.'

She got up. She looked angry now, but was fighting hard for control. Her nerves betrayed themselves in the jerky way she was puffing at her cigarette. 'I fail to see why I should put up with this insolence, Mr. Maclean,' she snapped. 'Who are you to come here and question me like this?'

'A private dick,' he told her. 'And I didn't come — you brought me, remember?'

'That may be. But unless you leave immediately, I shall call the servants and have you thrown out! Why, I wouldn't put up with this kind of thing from — from Dick Tracy himself!' She reached over towards a bell push, then paused.

'Go ahead and press,' invited Maclean. 'Then start figuring out what you're going to tell the servants about how I got here.'

'Will you go, Mr. Maclean? You're incredibly boring!'

'So are you, sister.' Maclean moved to her side and looked down into her eyes. They were veiled and hostile. 'So you can't say anything about this Forester sap?'

'No, nothing.'

'Very well. Maybe I can get him to sing, with a little effort. Maybe he had a hand in the disappearance and you're covering up for him. Could that be it?'

She sat up straight and looked at him. 'For the last time, why not forget Melanie Grant? What is she to you?'

'That's my affair.'

'And you're determined to see this man Forester?'

'I am. Right now, lady. We'll get to the bottom of this damned mystery if we take the rest of our lives to do it.'

'That might not be so long.'

'That's fighting talk. So you *do* know something?'

'I've told you, no. And I would advise you strongly to forget all about Melanie now, at once. Otherwise something very unpleasant might happen to you, Mr. Maclean,'

Maclean reached for his hat and crammed it on the back of his skull. He said: 'Don't bother to show me out. I'll manage!'

'You're going?'

'I told you I was, didn't I? There's nothing else for me here, is there?'

'Isn't there?' She was putting on the old sex act again, but Maclean wasn't to be shaken this time. He knew from her attitude that she suspected his visit to Forester might reveal things; things she didn't seem to want revealed.

'There's no use in talking anymore,' he said. 'If you won't spill what you know, I'll get it from Forester.'

'And suppose he won't talk either?'

'Then,' said Maclean, pausing with one hand on the doorknob, 'I'll be back to get it out of you, one way or another.'

'Maybe you won't get the chance, Mr. Maclean,' she said. And then he was gone; and with an angry, alarmed exclamation, Maisie Fredericks turned towards the telephone.

★　★　★

It was late, but Maclean flagged a cab and gave Forester's home address, which he had obtained from a phone book earlier. The cab decanted him at the entrance to an impressive residence, which was now wrapped in darkness and desolation. He walked through the open gates and trod up the drive.

It was late to start investigating, but the way Maisie Fredericks had reacted to his conversation with her had convinced him Forester knew something important. He was determined to strike while the iron was hot, and before they could get in touch with Forester, if he was in on whatever was going on.

He rang the bell at a massive door, and waited. It was opened to him by a staid and elderly butler. He was attired in comfortable flannel pyjamas; but his elbows, which he held akimbo, gave away his status.

'Yes, sir?' He was quite composed, and betrayed no irritation at being roused halfway through the night.

'I want to see Mr. Forester,' Maclean told him. 'Mr. Michael Forester.'

'I regret, sir, that Mr. Forester has long ago retired. I could hardly venture to disturb him now.'

'*I'll* disturb him,' grunted Maclean.

'You just tell him I'm waiting to see him.'

'But sir — '

'Tell him, fancy pants! And mention the name Melanie Grant to him. It should bring him. Now blow. I'll wait inside here.'

'If you insist, sir. Very well. Perhaps you would care to wait in the library?'

He led Maclean across a parquet floor and ushered him into the library. Maclean skimmed his eyes round the lines of books, then walked over to the curtained French windows and took a look out, but the grounds were invisible in the inky blackness. He turned back again, poured himself a drink from a decanter, and sat down in a large plush chair.

Soon the library door opened, and a thin, wizened old man came in. His chin was weak; so weak that had it not been for his gash of a mouth, it would have been indistinguishable from his throat. Thinning grey hair hung in fringes round his ears, and his yellow-skinned hands were working nervously as he entered the room.

'What does this mean?' the man asked.

'I'm Maclean — private investigator,' the detective told him.

'You — you mentioned the name — the name Melanie Grant to — to my servant?'

'That's so. Sit down and we can talk.'

'But — '

'Sit *down*. Now, let's not hold out on each other. I'll give you what I know, and you can fill the blanks. This Melanie Grant vanished a while ago, didn't she? You were seen with her a lot, and that puts the eight-ball from my point of view. Also, a certain Mrs. Fredericks thinks you know something. Now, you give?'

'Really, I don't understand. I did accompany Miss Grant once or twice, yes, when she worked at the — the Golden Garter Club. But that was so long ago now. I — I haven't seen her for so long. I can't really recollect what she was like, even.'

'But you were seeing her clear up to the time she vanished! And if she hadn't vanished, you'd most likely have gone on seeing her. Then doesn't it seem queer that you shouldn't bother yourself about her disappearance? If you were interested at all in her, you'd have wanted to know. Obviously you didn't!'

'She was merely an acquaintance.'

'It's no use — come clean, Forester. I'll have it sooner or later, so you may as well start squawking right now!'

Forester licked lips that were suddenly dry. His little eyes darted around the room and came back to Maclean. The detective knew he was weakening.

'I told you,' Foster managed in a thin voice.

'And I tell you I know you're holding something back. Let's hear it — or when I find out later, it'll be the worse for you! And I do find things out eventually. Maybe you've heard of me; Al Maclean's the name.'

The little man's hands twitched convulsively. 'Yes, I've heard of you, Mr. Maclean.'

'You know I don't flop any cases I take?'

'I know that, too. Very well, I'll tell you what I know. It will give you rather a shock, but then sooner or later I'll have to report it. I can't go on like this much longer, so perhaps this is as good a time as any. But I will ask you to give me your word that you will see no harm comes to me.'

'I'll take care of that,' Maclean agreed eagerly. He hadn't thought this would be so easy.

Forester rose nervously from his chair. 'I'll feel a lot easier if I draw the shutters on these windows. It's unlikely, but one never knows who may be lurking in the grounds.' He crossed to the window and began to draw the shutters. 'You must protect me, Mr. Maclean, when I have divulged what I know. God knows I'll need help. It all began when I met Melanie Grant one night at the Golden Garter Club. I thought then that she was a sweet, innocent woman who had been forced to turn to stripping to make a living. It was not until later — '

There was a sudden tinkle of glass. Forester stopped talking and raised one hand dazedly to his head. Then he half-spun towards Maclean, mouth and face working horribly. The neat round hole in his forehead told Maclean more than the man himself could have done!

Even as Forester's knees buckled, the detective was jumping across the room towards him. But it was useless — the man was dead!

In answer to Maclean's appearance at the window, glass shattered again, and he felt the whirr of bullets streaking past his head. He ducked, and heard a vase shatter across the room. He lay there for several minutes, watching the trickling line of blood from Forester's head as it crept sluggishly across the parquet.

When he finally rose, Maclean kept clear of the window. He knew it would be useless looking for the attacker out there in the pitch darkness. He hesitated, gazing down at the limp figure. Then he crossed to a nearby desk.

It was locked. Maclean didn't worry about that. His master keys never left his inner pocket. The third one fitted, and the lid of the bureau swung upward. His keys came into play on the top document drawer. It was full of old papers, but it only took Maclean's trained eye seconds to see they had no bearing on the case.

He tried the other drawers systematically. In the back corner of the bottom one, he found two unusual things. One was an old checkbook, containing stubs. The checks had been made out to a Miss N. Nilo — twenty of them, at 5000 dollars a time!

The other was a note, which said simply: 'You have fallen behind with your payments again. Unless you remedy this, certain facts concerning a certain strip-tease lady will come to light!' It was signed — Nita Nilo!

5

The Mysterious Miss Nilo

It almost made Maclean's brain reel, that note!

Blackmail? For what? Five thousand dollars a month, according to the checkbook. That was blackmail of the highest order — Forester must have done something extremely bad to pay that much for it to be hushed up. Something concerning Melanie Grant! There could be no doubt of the strip dancer to whom the note alluded. Somehow, somewhere, the Nita Nilo of the note had found out the hotel magnate's guilty secret, and had been bleeding him in the best tradition of blackmail. Yet Forester, apparently, had been about to talk to Maclean about Melanie Grant. He had been murdered at that precise moment!

What did that signify? Had Forester perhaps got the Grant woman into some kind of trouble, and then killed her? And this Miss Nilo had found out and blackmailed him with the threat of exposure? That certainly seemed the most likely theory. And yet, would Forester have confessed his crime to a private detective, even to avoid his extortionate payments? It would have meant the chair for Forester, and Maclean could not see a man with Forester's money risking the chair to avoid paying a meagre five thousand a month. Perhaps he had been going to spin some story that would implicate Miss Nilo, and not himself. But then, if Forester was the guilty person, why should he have been killed like that? The murder must have a bearing on the case; it would be far too big a coincidence if it hadn't.

And where did Maisie Fredericks come into it? That thought brought Maclean a possible — even probable — solution. Could it be that Maisie Fredericks was Miss Nilo? Did she know about Forester having murdered her friend, and was she obtaining money in that way? That would account for her reluctance to tell Maclean anything — more than account for it! It would also explain why she had been so perturbed by his threat to force a confession out of Forester, and her remark that perhaps the detective would not be coming back. The moment he had left her place, she could have followed on his heels, sneaked into the Forester grounds, waited for the opportunity, and shot the old man with a silenced revolver.

Yet at the same time, it struck Maclean that this scenario was hardly probable. If Forester had murdered his inamorata, surely Maisie would never have expected him to reveal the fact?

Maclean suddenly realised he was standing in the middle of a fashionable library, with the blood-smeared corpse of a prominent businessman lying before him! The thought electrified him into action. There was no danger immediately; but he assumed the butler would still be waiting to let him out, and the man might have heard the tinkle of falling glass and the thud of his master striking the floor. He might be getting, as it were, curiouser and curiouser, and Maclean had no intention of being there when his curiosity resolved itself into investigation. That wouldn't do at all. The police had a down on Maclean already, and this would clinch it for them: operating without a licence, found in a room alone with a murdered man! It would be exceedingly awkward.

The darkness of the grounds beyond the window beckoned invitingly to Maclean. He took a last look at the body, stuffed the check stubs and the note into his pocket, slid the window catch silently and ducked out, his body tensed to dive flat if there was any shooting.

There wasn't. The killer, of course, would not have expected him to exit that way. He was probably miles away now, gloating over a successful night's work. But he still hadn't got Maclean!

The detective started threading his way through the shrubbery, making for the gates. The police would arrive as soon as the body was discovered and the call had been put through — Maclean hoped the butler hadn't had a good enough look at him to identify him or at least to give a full and accurate description. If he had, it would be too bad. At least he didn't know the name — Maclean never gave that if he could help it.

He started walking back from Park Avenue to the Rose Graham Hotel. Time had passed more quickly than he had thought, and an early dawn was creeping over the sleeping city. An all-night milk wagon rumbled past with a sleepy driver at the wheel, and Maclean ducked into the shadows. It was casual evidence like that milkman might supply, if he saw Maclean, that had sent more than one man to the chair.

Maclean breathed deeply when he was clear of the scene of the murder. From an all-night eatery the clatter of pots and pans made itself heard, and since there were quite a few folks there he decided he might as well have a snack. He ate ham, eggs, french fries, and a good strong cup of black coffee. Then, over a thoughtful cigarette, he sat back to give the night's happenings his undivided attention.

Try as he would, however, he failed to figure out any angle other than the one that had suggested itself to him in Michael Forester's death chamber. He gave it up at last and ventured into the streets again. Inside ten minutes he was back at the hotel, up in his room, examining the note again. It showed him nothing. It was typewritten, and even the possibility of identifying the machine that had written it had been wiped out, for it had obviously been done on several different machines to eliminate that possibility. He could tell that from the different types of lettering — for instance, one G had a large loop; the one next to it a smaller one.

He sighed and stuffed the note in his wallet, then had a second look through the checks. Yes, they were all made payable to N. Nilo. Seemingly Forester had kept this book especially for her, not wishing to mix the amounts up with his legitimately drawn checks.

Maclean murmured to himself: 'Where do we go from here?' and didn't get any answer. He tossed off his clothing and climbed into his bed; he was tired, and he reckoned he'd need that sleep. Tonight he'd see Maisie Fredericks again, and perhaps he might even try a little blackmail himself. If she still refused to talk, he could always threaten to expose her little games to her doting husband. That might move her.

'Get up!'

The voice came harshly, shatteringly, into Maclean's sleep-crowded mind. It was a rough voice, uncultured, and it sounded as if it meant business. The hand that jarred his shoulder matched up with the voice.

He dragged himself back from dreamland and stared at the two men who were standing above his bed. He rubbed his eyes, blinked and stretched. 'Well, boys? I'd have locked my door if I'd known there were scavengers about.'

'Get up,' snarled the man nearest, menacing a gun at him. 'And get dressed. You're wanted!'

Maclean yawned and sat up. 'I make a point of never rising until I've had a cup of coffee in bed.'

'You'll get more'n coffee if you don't make it snappy,' grunted the second man.

'Remember the Dempster dame? Maybe we'll give you the same treatment we gave her!'

'You blasted fool,' grated the gun-holder. 'Can't you keep that big rat trap shut? We'll fry because of you one day!'

The second man coloured redly and opened his mouth — then shut it as if he had thought better of it. But Maclean remembered! Grace Baxter Dempster, daughter of the famous Dempster who owned Hollywood's largest studios — she had been found horribly beaten up in her apartments not a month ago.

'So you boys killed the Dempster woman? Why?'

'That needn't matter to you,' snapped the first man. 'Get going, quick!'

Maclean crawled out of bed and started to dress slowly. The two men stood watching him, jerky with impatience. 'What'll I wear?' he said. 'Is this meeting going to be formal, or will any old thing do?'

'Maybe it'll help if you've got a nice shroud to put on,' leered the second man, and Maclean knew he wasn't kidding. He put on an old pin-striped suit; he reflected that if this was really it, and he was due to be bumped off this time, there was no sense in having his best suit ruined. Maybe Good Time Rosie could find some hard-up actor who'd be glad of his good clothes!

While he dressed, he studied the two thugs carefully. One — the one who held the gun — was short and dark, and looked Italian. The fact that his companion addressed him as 'Ricky' didn't do anything to disclaim the assumption. The loud-mouthed specimen was about eight inches taller than his companion, and had a mouth that reached from ear to ear. His nose was a strawberry mass of red pockmarks, and his ears resembled nothing so much as a couple of deformed cauliflowers. Ricky referred to him as 'Nose', and Maclean wasn't surprised, for no other name could have done him justice unless it had been 'Ears'. He was nervier than Ricky: his fingers twitched continually, but his eyes had the glassy shine of a homicidal maniac. Maclean decided he could be very dangerous, and the very fact that he was obviously afraid of Ricky spelled that Ricky was even more to be watched.

'Speed it up,' grunted Ricky. 'Someone's waiting for you.'

'Who?'

'You'll find out soon enough. We got a car waiting, so's you don't get too tired for what's coming to you.'

'I don't suppose you'd let me in on our destination?'

'I don't see why not. We're taking a run downtown — business district. That's all.'

'What's the business?'

'That can wait, too. You ready?'

Maclean sighed and nodded, making a furtive attempt to slide his revolver into his breast pocket. It didn't work.

Ricky said: 'You won't need that, pal,' and gave him such a crack across the hand with the barrel of his gun that Maclean thought his fingers were busted.

Ricky slid his rod in his pocket. 'Listen — you're walking out of here by my side. I'll keep you covered through my pocket, and one yip out of you and I'll let you have it, don't make no mistake. I've heard a thing or two about you, an' if I did shoot you I'd be doin' every racketeer in the States a favour — so I won't hesitate.'

'You won't have to shoot, Trigger-Itch,' Maclean told him. 'I'll go quiet. In fact, I was just wondering what I was going to do to keep myself amused this afternoon — you found out for me.'

Ricky grunted, and with one heavy on each side, Maclean got going. They negotiated the first landing in silence; and as they walked along the second, a room door opened and a face looked out.

It was Gail Grant.

When she saw Maclean, she smiled, and came out. 'Oh, Al — I hoped I'd see you. Rosie told me you went out again last night, and I wanted to talk with you. Only you didn't get back until so late, I thought you weren't coming at all. I hope nothing happened?' She glanced dubiously at the two thugs with Maclean.

The detective grinned. 'Nothing happened, baby. Only I'm rather busy right now. I have to go with these gentlemen on a little matter of business, you see. Maybe I'll call on you when I get back.'

'Yeah, do that,' said Nose impatiently. 'Blow, sister. This guy has to come along with us.' And they hustled Maclean towards the stairs, leaving Gail staring after them with a white, worried face.

There was a car drawn up near the entrance; nothing pretentious — just a modest little jalopy that looked as if it belonged to any peace-loving city family. They herded Maclean into the back; Nose took the wheel, and Ricky kept the detective covered. The car moved away.

And now Maclean *was* on his own; he didn't for one minute think that the two hoods were taking him to downtown Manhattan. He thought they were running him to some lonely road, then giving him a lead lunch. Therefore he was extremely surprised when the car shot down towards the business section of the city. He said sarcastically: 'Fancy! I guess you've got an office also?'

'That's just what we have got, pal.' Ricky grinned. 'That's where we're headin' right now. We do things in style, see. The boss is plenty clever, and also plenty ritzy. Maybe you won't think she's very different from any other dame, but believe me, pal, she can be a hell cat when she likes — an' she very often does like!'

'Your boss is a woman?' asked Maclean, whistling.

'Sure. And in case that smile you've put on means you think you can put something over on her, get yourself straightened out right now. She wants to see you, bad — but when she's seen you, I can promise you'll get yours — you're getting under her feet, and nobody does that.'

'How am I getting under her feet?'

'She'll straighten you out on that. Personally I'm dead set against bothering with you at all — I would prefer to perforate a coupla lead pills through your carcass and let it go at that. But for some reason she wants to see you, so here you are.'

'You're lucky — I almost got perforated last night by some person or persons unknown.'

'They ain't unknown. The Nose was the guy who tried to bullet you.'

'Yeah? Then he shot Forester?'

'Sure — it won't hurt to tell you now

about that. If you'd been bumped last night, we wouldn't have this trouble. But the boss figures you may have found something out and told someone. That's why she's gotta see you.'

The car drew up outside an imposing block of offices. They got out and took a lift to the fifth, then went into an office. There was a woman behind a desk there with black hair pulled into a bun and horn-rimmed gig-lamps. If Maclean hadn't known any better, he would have thought he was being introduced to a librarian.

She stood up and said: 'Mr. Maclean? My name is Nita Nilo.'

6

Maclean Sees Below the Surface

Maclean gazed at her, startled. From all the novels he had ever read, she should have been beautiful and regal. Yet there was some grace and poise in the slender black-clad body, and some delicious shaping under the thick half-wool half-silk stockings. Maclean didn't miss it — nor did he miss her clear, lovely complexion and the brightness of her eyes. The eyes were startling: they didn't fit in that sombre setting at all.

She said: 'You seem to be speechless, Mr. Maclean. Perhaps if I were to send away my assistants, we could get along better.'

'Maybe we'd better stay,' began Nose.

She turned her gaze on him coldly. 'I'll give the orders, Nose. Is he armed?'

'Nuts,' Ricky told her. 'You don't figure we'd lug him around hipped up, do you?'

'Then you may leave us alone for a few minutes. I'll call when I want you again. Stay in the outer office.' She slid a small thirty-two from a desk drawer as they left reluctantly, then laid it before her on the desk. She rummaged in a drawer for a cigarette case, found it, and offered Maclean one.

'No, thanks. I'm rationing myself — got a smoker's cough.' He said that because he didn't trust her, and she knew it. She wanted to question him, and Maclean had been slipped drugged cigarettes before; they took your mental faculties away and left you an automatic question box, blindly revealing your innermost thoughts.

'Your smoker's cough doesn't matter now, Maclean. It won't trouble you very much longer — Ricky will take care of that. Still, if you're convinced I'm trying to poison you . . . ' She shrugged and lit one of the smokes herself. It was a further incongruity — that lighted cigarette tucked between lips innocently devoid of lipstick, in a calm, composed face that might have belonged to a vicar's prim daughter.

'You wanted me?'

'I did,' she assented. 'You have seen fit to interest yourself in my affairs — why?'

'That's my business.'

'Not any longer.'

'By your affairs, do you mean Forester, and the mystery surrounding Melanie Grant's disappearance?'

'Exactly. What else would I mean? Miss Grant has been missing a long time now. Why have you suddenly started to take notice of one insignificant woman in a city where thousands vanish every year?'

'I'm nosey.'

'You certainly are. But even a private detective would hardly start running around looking for one particular missing person unless he had good reason — unless someone were paying him for it.'

Maclean smiled. 'I expect your mind doesn't run any further than money, and I guess you wouldn't expect to find a philanthropic shamus. If you told me I'd be doing a job out of the goodness of my own heart, a week ago I'd have told you to get your bumps read. But that's a fact

— I'm doing this job to help someone who not only can't pay me, but also who doesn't mean a goddam thing to me.'

'I don't believe that.'

'You can believe what you like and go to hell.'

She twisted her swivel chair towards him. He sat on the edge of the desk and looked at her legs. The longish skirt had pulled far above her knees in her concentration on grilling him, and he saw another incongruous feature now. Above the tops of those thick, plain stockings, a hint of lacy pinkness peeked coyly out at him from a pair of wide-legged panties. And Maclean knew surely that that was the real woman showing through for him to see! That was the Nita Nilo of perfume and silk, of soft firm flesh, of tantalizing seductiveness! He sensed it even as he turned his gaze to her face and said: 'You mean to bump me off?'

'I do — or rather, to have Ricky do it for me.'

'Then why not get it over with? Why waste my time and yours in asking questions I haven't any intention of answering?'

'I'm curious, that's all.'

'You had some hand in Melanie Grant's death?'

'Death?' repeated the woman softly. 'Yes, Melanie Grant is dead! Dead and buried!'

'You killed her?' Maclean said. It was more a statement than a question, and the woman he knew as Nita Nilo nodded.

'I was responsible for what happened to her,' she admitted. 'But once again, why should that concern you or anyone else?'

Maclean didn't answer that one. He took a cigarette from his own case, lit it, and drew on it thoughtfully. 'Since I'm due to die anyway, what's the idea of not being yourself?'

'I don't understand you.'

'No? Well in the, first place, women like you're pretending to be — plain Janes — are never at the root of any organisation like you seem to have. Then again, I know your racket's blackmail — I found your note and Forester's check book last night. That doesn't tie in with your present appearance! Those lace doodads you're wearing aren't in keeping,

71

either.' Here she hastily adjusted her skirt. 'And,' concluded Maclean, 'you not only smoke, but you paint your fingernails and pluck your eyebrows! Come out of hiding, sister, and maybe I'll tell you what I know.'

She looked at him in surprise for a moment. Then she said: 'You're quite right, Maclean. Clever of you. This is merely my professional guise. But of course you'd naturally see through it, wouldn't you? You're a smart detective, and you look through the veneer and see the type of wood beneath.'

'Not exactly the *wood*,' said Maclean with a grin, eyeing her legs.

She stood up, and without speaking she took a slide from her hair at the back, then shook the long tresses over her shoulders. They fell into curving waves; a glossy black mass of silken strands. Next she removed the horn-rimmed spectacles, and her eyes burst from behind them twice as brilliant, twice as alluring. From a handbag she took lipstick and powder and rouge; within a minute the change was unbelievable. Gone was the woman of the plain style Maclean had recently watched. In her place stood a tall voluptuous creature, dark of eye and hair, with a warm swelling bosom and beautifully moulded hips. Even the drab black dress and thick stockings failed to conceal the natural beauty of her figure. It was, reflected Maclean, like a butterfly emerging from a cocoon. No, not a butterfly — a dragonfly perhaps. For there was an air of menace about her, despite her smile.

'And now that you have the reality?'

'I am more than satisfied,' conceded Maclean. 'And since you have pandered to my curiosity, I can do hardly more than satisfy yours. I have said I am being philanthropic in taking this case, and that is perfectly true. My reason for doing so is a young lady called Gail Grant — the kid sister of that woman you admit to killing.'

'What!'

For a moment he thought she would collapse, such was her emotion. She stood with one hand tightly gripping the edge of her desk; her knuckles showed white under the strain. Her eyes searched his face desperately, as if looking for a sign that he was speaking the truth. At last, in a husky voice, she said: 'It — it's impossible! That — Melanie Grant's sister is — is still in her home town. I — '

'It's true, and it'll be easy for you to verify.'

'You mean — you mean that to help this — this Gail Grant, you'd run all this risk?'

'I didn't know how much risk there'd be when I started, but now it's too late to turn back. Besides, the kid was alone and in trouble — she was mixed up with a dirty knife-throwing swine called Salato when I met up with her. I was lucky enough to save her from him, but I couldn't have spent all my time looking after her. Seemingly her folks died and she made the trip here to join her sister, Melanie, then found that Melanie didn't live here anymore. So I told her I'd look around and see what I could do.'

Nita Nilo had taken a firmer grip on herself now. 'I think I believe you. How is Melanie's sister?'

'Gail? She's fine — only the kid hasn't

much dough, and she won't last long in New York. She doesn't know how to look after herself yet.'

'And that is your sole reason for — for investigating the missing Melanie Grant?'

'It is. What other reason would I have?'

She lit a further cigarette and looked at him hard. She said: 'Mr. Maclean, I admire you. Very much. I thought private detectives had hearts only one degree softer than stone. I was wrong, in your case.'

'Thanks,' he told her. 'It's nice to know, but it won't make it any less pleasant when the slugs hit me.'

She made a sudden decision. 'They aren't going to hit you. I've changed my mind. If you will give me your word you won't permit this incident, or anything you have yet found out about the missing Melanie Grant, to go any further, I will turn you free here and now.'

Maclean could only stare at her. She repeated impatiently: 'Well? Do you give your word, or must I get Ricky to carry out your execution?'

'Lady, you have my Wolf Cub's

honour,' said Maclean. 'But why the change of heart?'

She didn't seem to hear him make that remark. She went on: 'You agree to drop the investigation, of course?'

'No,' he told her flatly. 'I do not. I merely agree not to let any of my findings go any further. As for me — I guess I'll stick right in there, looking for that missing kid!'

'And when you've found — found out what became of her?'

'I'll figure that when the time comes.'

'You won't communicate with the police?'

'Not until I'm certain. They kinda suspended my licence — they don't know I'm still operating.'

She smoothed her dress over her thighs and said: 'Mr. Maclean, will you do me the honour of dining with me tonight?'

It was another surprise. Maclean was suspicious. He said: 'Why?'

'I may be able to make it worth your while to drop the case.'

'I don't think so — but you can try, I guess. How about the Golden Garter Club?'

'No — no, not there. Shall we say the Starlight Roof at the Waldorf? Seven-thirty?'

'I'll be there,' he agreed. 'White tie and tails.'

'Perhaps we'll reach an understanding.'

Maclean decided he'd better straighten her out right away. 'I don't reach understandings with murderesses, lady. I'll be along because I'm still nosey, and I may find out a thing or two. I don't know why you suddenly decided to let me live, but anyway I'm thanking you for it, without changing any of my opinions about you.'

She looked at him questioningly: 'Which are?'

'That you're a swell looker — swell! And you've a figure that'd make a guy wonder what he ever saw in Dorothy Lamour that you haven't got twice as much of. But that you're as dangerous as a rattlesnake, and as mean as any skunk that ever walked. I know you had a big hand in whatever happened to Melanie Grant — and when I finally know for sure, look out for yourself.'

She smiled at him, unruffled, and sneered: 'You're exactly like a movie detective, Maclean. Who gave you lessons? Lloyd Nolan?'

'Cut the funny cracks. If you haven't killed any poor sap yourself, you've had it done. I guess Lucretia Borgia hadn't a thing on you — at least she made love to 'em before she did the job!'

'And what makes you think I don't?'

Maclean snorted. 'How much longer you going to keep me here? Do I go, or don't I? I'm getting tired of being clever.'

'I'd like to ask you just one thing more,' she told him. 'If Melanie Grant had wanted to vanish — to die I might say, even; if it had been her dearest wish that no one should try to find out what had become of her — what would you say then?'

'I'd say you were lying. And it isn't only her. Forester, the Dempster dame, and how many more? What is your racket, sister?'

'Only blackmail, Maclean. The Dempster woman threatened to expose us, and Ricky and Nose lost their nerve and killed her. I can assure you I was very angry with them for it. She wouldn't have talked.'

'And Forester?'

'He was weak. I think he would have talked to you. That's why he had to go.'

'How did you know I was seeing him? Who gave you that information? Maisie Fredericks? Where does she come into this?'

'Really! I brought you here to ask you the questions. As for the woman you mention, I never even heard of her.'

'No? You're lying again. Can't you ever tell the truth, sister?'

' 'If to her lot some female errors fall',' she quoted with modesty, ' 'look on her face, and you'll forget them all!' Pope, Mr. Maclean — or didn't your education carry you that far?'

'Further — 'Men some to business, some to pleasure take, but every woman is at heart a Rake!' *Also* Pope, lady.'

She smiled and pressed a button on her desk. Ricky and Nose entered. Nose said eagerly: 'We bump him now, boss?'

She ignored him, turned to Ricky and

said: 'Take him back to the hotel. See that no harm comes to him.'

'But . . . ' began Ricky, then stopped as he caught her look.

At the door she said: 'You won't forget our — date?'

'No,' Maclean told her. 'But there's one thing — for God's sake, change that blasted dress!'

7

Strange Meeting

All the way home, Maclean's mind buzzed. Certainly Miss Nilo had denied all knowledge of Maisie Fredericks, but Maclean didn't for one instant take her statement at face value. It all tied in too neatly. He had not decided to go to Forester's home until a few moments prior to leaving Maisie's place — she was the only one who could possibly have known his intentions. There was ample time for her to telephone Miss Nilo and arrange a pleasant surprise for him! It fitted; and Maclean wondered what part Maisie Fredericks played in the game.

At the hotel he found Gail in a frenzy of worried impatience. Her relief at his return was evident, and Maclean felt elated at her concern for him. It was novel to really mean something to someone — there were so few people

Maclean meant *anything* to.

But as he talked with her, carefully refraining from upsetting her by informing her of anything that had so far occurred, his thought was of Miss Nilo and the date for that evening. He wondered what the woman was driving at now. He also wondered if he would be wise to go — then told himself that if she wanted to kill him, it could have been just as easily done that very day when he had been in her hands. No — the Starlight Roof at the Waldorf was far too crowded a location for murder!

A plan was forming in his mind: it might tell him nothing, or it might tell him a lot. The idea was to confront Nita Nilo with Maisie Fredericks and see if, by glance or word, they betrayed any connection. But he would have to leave it late, otherwise the two could get in touch. He would have to wait until the last possible moment before issuing an invitation to Maisie.

He did. It was seven o'clock before he telephoned her at her home, and was lucky enough to be put on to her right away.

'Maclean speaking,' he told her. 'I just wondered what you were doing tonight.'

Her voice, faintly surprised, came through: 'Mr. Maclean? Really! I thought that after last night — '

'I know, I know. I changed my mind — it's a detective's privilege. I wondered if you'd dine with me tonight?'

'Well, I did have another date.'

'You did? I'm sorry. He'll be disappointed, won't he?'

A faint ripple of laughter came to his ears. 'You're incorrigible, Al! Yes, I think he will!'

'Swell — I'll pick you up at your address at seven-thirty. Can you make it?'

'Easily. I'm already dressed. I'll cancel the other appointment.'

'It'll be all right to pick you up at home?'

'Perfectly. My husband knows I'm quite trustworthy. The perfect model of fidelity, in fact.' There was that sneer in her voice as she said it.

He said: 'Expect me in the half-hour — and thanks.' Then he hung up, donned coat and hat, and went along to the nearest saloon for a few quick ones before the evening commenced. He looked forward to the evening — it promised to be interesting indeed.

At seven-thirty-one precisely, Maisie Fredericks answered the door to his knock. She seemed rather surprised to see that he had walked, and that there was no cab waiting. She said: 'Didn't you bring a taxi-cab, Al?'

'No; I figured we'd use your husband's car. He can afford it better than I can, and it's only fair he should stand part of the racket if I'm going to entertain his wife!'

'At least you're original.' She chuckled as she handed him a fur cape to hold. 'Where are we going?'

'The Starlight at the Waldorf,' he informed her, and she nodded as if to say she approved of his choice. A luxurious car and chauffeur awaited them at the door, and Maclean packed himself into it while she went to say so long to her bed-ridden husband. She came back in a few seconds, smiling.

Maclean said: 'All right?'

'Of course. He told me to be sure I had a good time. When I told him my escort was a private detective, he said how adventurous, and he supposed it was very romantic, me going out with a private detective. He said he'd heard things about them, but he knew I could look after myself.'

'He's a sap,' said Maclean, and would have liked to have found a more appropriate word, but couldn't.

★   ★   ★

The light grey, forty-seven-story Waldorf-Astoria thrust itself up from Park Avenue into the summer night. The Starlight Roof was doing its usual crowded summer business, and the movable roof was opened to the brilliance of a cloudless star-studded sky. Immaculate waiters, an imperturbable maître d'hôtel, energetic elevator operators, bus boys, chefs, assistant chefs, waiter's captains, vegetable cooks, a coffee man, a buffet man, a vegetable woman, a clerk, a toast woman, an ice man, a barman, a coordinating steward, a storeroom clerk, bus women, a service elevator starter, a kettle washer, a pot washer, and a glass washer all bustled about energetically, pandering to the catholic tastes of the wealthy who dined in that superbly appointed room which was the Starlight Roof at the Waldorf-Astoria.

Miss Nilo had secured a table on the right-hand side of the band, on the edge of the infinitesimal section of space reserved for the dancer-diners. Her eyes flickered brightly over the crowded floor, searching for Maclean. He was late, and she was getting impatient wondering if he really intended to keep that date.

A white-coated waiter slid over through the packed tables and said: 'Will madam order now?'

She shook her head. 'I'm waiting for a friend. He should be here directly.'

The waiter bowed and slid away again, navigating the diners with a skill that had taken long years of practice to accomplish. Miss Nilo allowed her gaze to wander about the room. She was waiting for Maclean, and the fear that he would not come was growing stronger within her. He *must* come, she told herself.

He did come, with Maisie Fredericks by his side, conducted to her table by an impressive head waiter. He said: 'Quite a night — sorry I'm late. Have you met Mrs. Fredericks? Hope you don't object to her joining us?'

As he spoke, he watched closely. The two women nodded distantly, as strangers might — except that the nod was far *too* distant. It looked as if it had been specially staged for Maclean's benefit! Also, he detected a hint of annoyance in Miss Nilo's eyes.

'Of course not.' She smiled, belying the look ineffectually. 'Please sit down, Mrs. Fredericks. I was about to order. Will you do it for me, Mr. Maclean?'

As he ordered, Maclean weighed her up. Her loveliness was now showing to the full. Her gown was a shimmering silver haze, cut low at the breast, and backless. Her smooth satiny skin glowed warmly beneath the shaded lights; and her features, touched by only a little make-up, made him think of rosy apples and jugs of thick cream. Even Maisie, voluptuous as she was, faded beneath the clean beauty of Miss Nilo. There were many beautiful women at the Starlight; many who earned their living by their looks — but not one could overshadow the woman before him, the woman he knew for a murderess and blackmailer, with a hard lump of granite instead of a heart.

Many of the celebrities glanced in their direction, and Maclean saw envy, admiration, and disapproval cast at her. He smiled and said: 'While we're waiting, shall we dance?'

She acquiesced with a nod of the head. Maisie was still sitting stupefied, taken aback by finding Miss Nilo there. As Maclean said 'Will you excuse us?', she threw him a glare of malice that fairly burned and blistered his face. Maclean noticed also that the look she gave Miss Nilo was no less savage. He had done a rotten thing, perhaps, to both of them. But if he could bring about an estrangement — assuming they *did* know each other — then something might be made out of it. He meant to try, anyway.

In a voice of acid sweetness, Maisie said: 'But of *course* I don't mind! I *love* to come to dinner with a man, then sit staring vacantly about while he dances with another woman.'

But they didn't hear her last remark; they were out on the floor, circulating about two inches to right and left, in a continuous monotonous shuffle which the Starlight Roof accepted for dancing.

The dance ended, and they returned to their table without Miss Nilo having spoken. Maclean knew she was annoyed; she showed it plainly. But once back there, she began to throw off her mood and laughed and chatted incessantly, making it impossible for Maclean to even notice Maisie's presence.

And Maisie was getting wilder and wilder. It happened when Maclean had excused himself for a moment: he was returning from the men's room and came upon the table unnoticed by the two women. They were talking together; and, coming up behind them, Maclean clearly heard Miss Nilo speaking.

'I tell you,' she hissed, 'you'll *have* to

leave! I have something very important to discuss with him — something private!'

'Damn you,' Maisie was saying vehemently, 'I won't go! I want him, and I'll *have* him, do you understand? If you think you can take him from me — '

'Don't be ridiculous,' Miss Nilo said distantly. 'You permit your desire to overrule your judgment. I merely want him for a matter of business. After tonight, you can have every inch of him — but not until I've finished this little matter off.'

'I don't believe that,' snapped Maisie. 'You'd better not start any funny stuff with me. I know too much about you!'

'Really. Aren't you being silly. Don't forget you're as much in it as me, will you?'

Maisie clenched her hands together and was silent.

Nilo continued: 'Please don't make a scene — go now.'

Without a further word, Maisie Fredericks rose, and, without seeing Maclean, began to thread her way through the tables towards the cloak room. Maclean waited a moment, watching Miss Nilo as she followed the other woman's progress with a frowning face. Then he coughed lightly and came to his own side of the table.

'Oh, there you are, Mr. Maclean. Your — er — lady friend had to leave, I'm afraid.'

'Had to?'

'Yes. I believe she was suffering from a headache. The noise, you know.'

'I see.'

'I'm rather tired myself. I'd like to have a word in private with you, too. I have a room here — if you'd come along, we could have a drink.'

Her room was three floors down; when they arrived, she locked the door behind them and said to Maclean: 'Quite cosy, isn't it? I took it especially for tonight.'

'I thought you had to make reservations to get a room here.'

'You do, but this room belongs to a — a person I know. When I asked him if I might use it — well, he didn't refuse.'

'I think I see. He *daren't* refuse,' said Maclean grimly.

'Put it like that if you wish.'

She sat down and patted the settee beside her. Maclean grunted and joined her. She poured drinks from a small table and gave him one. 'What is your opinion of me?' she said suddenly.

'I told you this afternoon. It hasn't altered any.'

'I don't mean my character. I mean my . . . physical attraction, shall we call it?'

'What's that to do with anything?'

'You don't understand what I'm driving at. Just answer my question. Suppose, for instance, I suggested an affair?'

'You're being too delicate for an uncouth private detective,' snapped Maclean. 'You mean, suppose you suggested us spending the night here.'

'If you wish. Will you?'

'I'll admit you're something for the boys; and I guess any other guy under the age of eighty would take up your offer. But not me. Maybe I'm nuts, but there it is.'

'You don't think I'm attractive?'

'It isn't that. You're just as attractive to me as a woman I once loved desperately.

It's just that your friend Maisie Fredericks tried the same game on me, and found it didn't work.'

'She isn't my friend,' retorted Miss Nilo. 'I told you I don't know her. But let's get back to the matter at hand. Is it that you don't trust me?'

'No; I've had to trust you so far, and there could be no harm in taking up your offer now. You're a swell looker, too. But I just don't happen to be that kind of a guy. You get me?'

8

Guilty Conscience?

'It doesn't worry me, what you think,' Maclean said, pouring himself another drink. 'I'm getting used to that line you pulled now, though I still can't understand it coming from you. You may be a damned hard-hearted woman, and a killer in the bargain, but I figured you'd kind of take care of yourself — you didn't seem the type to be mauled around.'

'I'm not. You still don't understand.'

'I don't want to. I guess I had you added up wrong, that's all. I didn't class you with the Fredericks floozie.'

'I should have hated it if you had. Maisie Fredericks can't help being the way she is.'

'So you *do* know her?'

Nilo bit her lip. 'I'd heard of her. But I'm not the same type; don't think it for a minute. I had a good motive for doing what I did.'

'You had?' Maclean said with a faint stirring of interest. 'What was it?'

'Listen — I think you'll agree that New York is no place for an innocent woman.'

That gave Maclean a belly laugh. 'You should worry!'

'I don't mean myself. Don't keep being funny; I know it's a front you put up. You don't really feel smart, do you?'

'No, I don't,' he told her frankly. 'I can't make out a damn thing about this case. I'm balled up, that's what.'

'And yet, if you only knew . . . It's quite simple. Maybe someday I'll tell you, but now I want you just to listen to me. You do agree that it isn't right for a young woman to be alone, making her way in New York?'

'I do. It's pleading for trouble.'

'That's right — and Melanie Grant's sister Gail has already run into one helping. If she's here unprotected much longer, she'll find some more — isn't that so?'

'That is so. But what's the point, lady?'

'The point is, she needs protection

— and such a man as yourself must give it to her. That's why I tried to get you to stay the night with me, so I'd know if you were a certain type of man. If you were, you'd have jumped at the chance.'

'And if I hadn't said no?'

'Then I'd have gone through with it. You're not unattractive in my eyes. But I would have known you weren't a fit man to do what I'm asking you to do.'

'Which is?'

'Look after Gail for a while, until she gets used to the city.'

Maclean didn't even laugh. The suggestion was so outrageous that he was stunned. Finally he said: 'I'm a detective, not a wet nurse.'

'A detective without a licence! And without too much money. I haven't exactly been idle since I last saw you. I know how you're placed.'

'It's a hopeless suggestion. Naturally I'd keep an eye on the kid, but I can't run her life. If she wants to go around with some wolf, who am I to say no?'

'You could do it. You could persuade her not to. And any woman with twenty

96

thousand dollars to her credit in the bank is going to have a whole lot of wolves circulating around her, isn't she?'

'*Twenty grand?* But the kid's almost penniless.'

'Not now. This afternoon, after you'd gone, I deposited twenty thousand dollars to her credit in the National. She's free to draw on it at once.'

'Why? Why should you do this for the sister of the woman you murdered? Tell me that.'

She shrugged and smiled a little. 'You don't credit me with having any good in me, do you? Suppose I did it because, but for me, the kid would have found her sister and been safe with her? Call it a guilty conscience, if you like.'

'You're still lying,' Maclean said. 'There's something at the bottom of all this. Suppose she wants to know where all that dough came from?'

'I've arranged with the bank manager to tell her that her sister left it lying there when she vanished, and that now they've found a relation they've arranged to turn it over to her.'

'You think she'll believe that?'

'Why not? She's only a kid, isn't she? She wouldn't know any better. She might wonder where her sister got it from, but it won't hurt her to wonder.'

'Twenty thousand!' whistled Maclean. 'Whew! She'll go completely crazy.'

'That's what I thought. That's why I'm having it left to her with you as trustee. She won't be able to draw a cent if you don't endorse the check.'

'What? Why, you're nuts.'

'No, I'm not, and I know you'll play fair. I've had details of your past record filched out. Rumour has it you're a swell fellow — sorry to embarrass you, but you must know it's true. You'll take the lady under your wing, Maclean, and look after her?'

'Why should I?'

'You would anyway — but you will now because ten thousand dollars has been deposited to your own credit at the same bank.'

Maclean didn't speak then; he had the feeling that if he did, he'd suddenly wake up and find himself smoking opium in some Bowery den. It all seemed like a pipe dream.

'You *will* look after her for a couple of years?'

'Lady,' said Maclean reverently, 'for ten thousand bucks I'd guarantee to keep Mae West out of trouble! But,' he went on quickly, 'I am not going to lay off the case. It is still my intention to find out what you did to this Melanie Grant, and why. Only now I'll have to figure out why you're so benevolent as well.'

'That's all right. I don't think you'll manage to find out very much about me. But if I know you're looking after Gail, I'll feel a lot happier about what I did to Melanie Grant.'

Maclean looked at her hard, then stood up and reached for his coat and hat, putting them on slowly. 'I guess I'll never get to the bottom of women. There's that Maisie Fredericks, quite willing to see me go to my death last night, and yet today she argues with you over who'll have me — sure, I overheard the both of you. It was Maisie who phoned you, wasn't it?' Because she said nothing, he went on:

'Here's how I figure it so far. When Maisie got hitched, somehow she contacted you. She married a wealthy socialite, which allowed her to move in higher circles. With her capacity for creating scandal herself, it wouldn't be hard for her to smell it out. She passed the tip to you, and you blackmailed the parties concerned. Melanie Grant, having been Maisie's roommate, got to know what was going on, and maybe threatened to expose the racket. So she was killed. Where Forester comes into it, I don't know, unless he was in with you. Yet he couldn't have been, because *he* was paying *you* blackmail money also. The only other solution is that he was carrying on an intrigue with Melanie, you tried to blackmail him, and she found out and said she'd expose you. That would explain why you bumped her, and why Fredericks told me he wanted protection if he talked. Is that it?'

'What do you think, Mr. Maclean? You seem to have it all worked out to your satisfaction.'

'Sure. There's only one point that

doesn't connect: if what I figure *is* right, how is it you're so worried about Gail Grant? You aren't the kind of woman to have any conscience.'

'Suppose Melanie Grant was working for me, getting suckers and handing me their letters to blackmail them with? Suppose she got killed while working for me? I'd feel a certain responsibility for her kid sister then, wouldn't I?'

Maclean shrugged. 'Not a woman like you. I guess they don't come any harder. No, there's something smelly someplace, and believe me I'll find out what. When I do, I'll be seeing you again! Don't think you've kidded me into thinking you're soft, sister. After what happened to that Dempster woman, and to Forester, and probably to a dozen or so more of your victims, I wouldn't *ever* think that. I think you're playing some deep game, but I'll get the dope on you; and when I do, we'll see just what the game is. In the meantime, I guess your dough's good, even if you did bleed some poor sucker white for it; and I'm taking your offer. So you needn't worry any about the kid. She'll be okay.'

He didn't say anything else. Miss Nilo thanked him in a low voice, and the detective almost thought she meant it. Then he had gone out of the room, leaving her sitting there, staring at the door.

She sat silent for about five minutes; then with a muffled sob she threw herself onto the settee, and tears streamed down her face as she cried: 'Oh, God! Why did I ever get myself into this sort of thing? He hates me and all my kind! Oh, if only I'd met him before — he'd have helped me to throw this game over, before it was too late . . .'

*   *   *

Maclean, walking home, had no idea that Miss Nilo was already in love with him. His thoughts were a confused mixture. He was thinking: Hell! Why does a woman like that have to be mixed up in dirty, stinking rackets? Why does it happen that way? And won't I ever meet up with anyone who attracts me and doesn't have anything to fear from the cops? Or is there something in the composition of a bad woman that attracts me naturally? God knows I always gravitate to the lowest quarter of any city I'm in. Could it be the same with women? Do I always pick the low ones?

Al Maclean, although he would not admit it to himself even, was feeling more than physical desire for Miss Nilo. He had thought once he could never love another woman after that certain Lala Cortini who had died for him. Now he knew he had been wrong — but he still thrust it from his mind savagely, for there could never be anything that would make Maclean overlook murder.

Or could there?

He reached the Rose Graham with his mind still in turmoil, and when he knocked at Gail Grant's door he tried to pull himself together. He'd promised to see her when he got back, and it was still very early. She opened the door to him, and she looked scared. Her blue eyes were wide and frightened, and her golden hair tumbled enchantingly about her shoulders. She held the negligee she wore tighter.

'Oh, come in Al, please. I'm so glad you're back. I was frightened. Terribly.'

Maclean smiled at her and went in. He sat on the edge of the bed and took the smoke she offered him. 'What of, kid? You've got nothing to worry about, have you?'

'It was Salato.'

'Salato? That dirty . . . ? What?'

'After you'd gone tonight, he came back for his things. His hand was bandaged. I met him on the landing, face to face.'

'He didn't . . . ?'

'No, he didn't speak to me. But — oh, Al, the look he gave me! I'm sure he'd kill me — and you too, if he could. It was an awful glare, like a wild beast! It frightened me.'

'Don't worry, honey. The louse had to come back for his clothes, that's all. We'll never hear from him again. Now I've some good news for you. It seems that before your sister vanished, she left a sum of money in the bank. They've decided to let you have it as her nearest living relative.'

In her innocence she took it all in, not even bothering to ask him how he had found out. She had complete faith in him, and Maclean felt rather a heel fooling her like he was. He went on: 'Twenty thousand dollars. There's only one thing: they've appointed me trustee. You won't mind that, will you?'

She laid her hand on his arm. 'There's no one I'd like any better. But Al, this doesn't mean that — that — that Melanie's — dead?'

He lied to her again. He couldn't bear the look in her eyes. He knew how tough it was to feel entirely alone in a big city, and how tough it was to lose your only living relative. 'No, no, it doesn't mean that, kid. Just means, well, they can't find her, you know, and she's been missing a long time. Don't go telling yourself anything bad's happened to her. Maybe she left town for some reason.'

'But why would she do that? And how did she get twenty thousand dollars?'

'Easily. It grows on trees in New York. A smart woman can always get good pickings. And as for running out of town, perhaps she got into a small jam down at the night club where she worked.'

'Night club? Melanie? But Al, she didn't work at a night club. In her letters to me she always said she was working as a waitress on Fifth Avenue!'

'Hell! Er, I meant down at the café, honey. They — waitresses — often get in jams.'

'You're not telling me the truth, are you, Al? You know she worked in a night club. She didn't want to tell me because I've always been prudish and easily shocked. What was she? Truthfully?'

'She was a — a strip-tease dancer, honey. But that's no sin.'

For a second Gail seemed shocked speechless. Then she smiled and said: 'I don't care what she was. I loved her. She was always a queen to me, and always will be.'

'Atta woman,' said Maclean, and squeezed her hand tightly. He left her soon after that, and to his embarrassment she kissed him good night. He went up to his room then, threw open the door and walked in.

'Hell!' he said. 'You boys again? What do you think this is, Grand Central Terminal?'

Ricky and Nose, Miss Nilo's lieutenants, detached themselves from the bed and levelled their guns at him. Ricky said: 'Don't try anything, Maclean. This is just a social call.'

9

Maclean, Burglar

Maclean wasn't very surprised; he had expected something of the kind, for earlier that day, when Ricky and Nose had found he was not to be bumped off after all, he had detected the sullenness on their faces. Obviously they considered him a menace to Miss Nilo and her organisation — a menace that would be better removed.

Ricky stood up and came over towards him. Nose put his gun away and frisked him. Then they indicated that he should sit on the bed, and he did, for he had a strong policy about arguing with forty-fives. He was about to work the old 'to what am I indebted' gag when Ricky saved him the trouble by saying: 'We're here to do you some good, smart guy — and if you're as smart as you're cracked up to be, you'll do like we say.'

'I'm all ears,' Maclean told him patiently. 'Though for the love of heaven I can't picture you guys in the roles of good Samaritans.'

'I ain't no S'maritan,' grunted Nose. 'I'm a good honest American, born and bred.'

'I believe the American part of it,' said Maclean. 'About the good and honest, I'm not so sure.'

Ricky said: 'We aren't here to waste time arguing with the sap, Nose. Just answer a question, Maclean.'

'That's all I seem to do on this case. Hell, I'm beginning to think everyone's a detective bar me! Okay, what's wrong?'

'Just what's with you and Miss Nilo?' demanded Ricky.

'How d'you mean, what's with us? I don't get you.'

Ricky scowled. 'You know what I mean. What makes with you? There's something mighty funny going on between you and that dame. We got a right to know what!'

'She's your boss, isn't she? Why not ask her?'

'We're askin' *you*. She pays us, but

don't get the idea we'd do just like she tells us if we thought she was throwing one over on us. We want to know why she suddenly released you after she said you'd haveta be bumped, why she fixed up to meet you tonight at the Waldorf, and why she's deposited big dough in the bank for you and some dame.'

'You boys find things out, don't you?' Maclean said.

'We keep our eyes an' ears open, sure. We have to. Now how about answering?'

'Sure. You see, she suddenly found out I was her long-lost son; that's all there is to it!'

Nose said: 'Geeze! Can ya imagine that?'

'Still being clever, eh?' Ricky said. 'Okay, if you like the knocks, pal. Nose, see what you can do.'

'But if the guy's her long-lost son — ' began Nose.

'You sap,' growled Ricky. 'I sometimes wonder if you don't still believe in Santa Claus!'

'You mean the guy's lyin'? I figured he was a bit old to be her son. Why, the crooked punk . . . '

Ricky said: 'One move from you, Maclean, an' I'll blast you. Now hit him, Nose!'

Nose lumbered forward and hit Maclean. Maclean took it full in the eyes and caromed backwards over the bed. It hurt like hell, and for several seconds he couldn't see a thing, and was only aware of a lancing agony behind the bridge of his nose. Then Nose kicked him in the groin for good measure, hard, and Maclean rolled under the bed, groaning.

'Get the yellow heel out of that,' grated Ricky. 'Hit him again, Nose, if he still ain't talking!'

Nose got hold of one of Maclean's legs and hauled. Maclean came out like a cork from a popgun, and Nose toed him as he rolled by. He panted for breath and gasped: 'Wait a minute — what do you want to know?'

'Why the boss gave you that dough. We don't know nothing about her past, and for all we know she might be pulling a fast one on us.'

'She gave it to me to — to lay off the

case,' Maclean said.

'An' you're laying off?'

'So help me. I wouldn't want to run up against you two boys again,' groaned Maclean, rubbing his nose.

Nose said: 'I don't get it — why didn't the boss just have you rubbed out? Why should she pay you good dough when a bullet only costs a coupla cents or so?'

'Maybe she likes me.'

Ricky said: 'Okay. We won't kill you this time, Maclean. But who's this dame she's paying dough to?'

'That I don't know. Ask her.'

'Maybe we will. And latch onto this, will ya — if we run into you again, you can start leavin' the dough she gave you to whoever you want to inherit it! Is that plain?'

'You won't run into me again, boys,' vowed Maclean. 'I think too much of my good looks.'

'Give him one last reminder, Nose,' Ricky said, and Nose started to come for Maclean.

By the time Maclean managed to straighten out again, the two hoods were gone. Gingerly the detective dragged himself onto the bed and lay there, his hands pressing hard into his groin. It was a long time before the pain eased down, but when it did he was as mad as a hornet. Far from frightening him off, the beating made him want to get right on with the case and put the two mugs where they couldn't do any further harm.

There was only one angle he could try now. Somewhere Miss Nilo must keep papers relating to the folks she black-mailed. And where other than in that office she owned? It was that simple, Maclean hoped. Probably she ran the place as a level business premises — maybe she had some front that was on the level, and the suckers went there and paid their dough when she demanded it. It was worth a try. Maclean picked himself up, drank some whisky neat, rubbed his face over with a damp cloth, and went to his trunk. From it he took a small tool kit, which he stuffed this inside his coat pocket. Then he donned a pair of sneakers, slid a loaded rod into his hip pocket, and left the hotel again.

He remembered exactly where the office was. The front of the building was locked and bolted up, but Maclean didn't let a small thing like that stop him. He manipulated with his keys, passed inside, and closed and locked the door after him.

He started walking up the stairs; he was halfway up when the sharp rays of a powerful flashlight cut against the wall on the next floor, and a voice called: 'Who's down there? Is there anyone down there?'

Footsteps commenced to descend the stairs, and Maclean tensed and crouched back. It must be the watchman, or night guard. He'd naturally think there were burglars on the premises.

Maclean drew back in the shadow of an office doorway and waited. A peaked cap came into view, followed by a burly beetle-browed character in a blue serge uniform. He bore a large service gun in one hand and a flashlight in the other. He descended carefully, the flashlight rays fixed right ahead.

Maclean tried to shove himself clear through the locked door behind him. The guard paused hardly two feet from

Maclean and peered down the staircase. He muttered to himself: 'Must have the jitters. Could have sworn I heard some noises on this landing.' He scratched his head, removing his peaked cap to do so, and Maclean saw his chance. He stepped out quickly and smacked the watchman on the rear of the neck with a ham-like fist. The blow had been perfectly placed, and the man went flat without a murmur.

Maclean grinned. 'Sorry, pal,' he said, and went on again, up the stairs to the fifth floor.

Miss Nilo's door was locked, but he had expected that. It didn't hold him any more than the main door had done. Within two minutes he was inside, fumbling in his pocket for his flashlight. The ray cut across the office and centred on a safe door he remembered seeing that day. He crossed the room and knelt by it.

'Damn it,' he muttered as he twiddled the combination. 'I can't work without a decent light.'

'This any better, pal?'

The office was suddenly flooded with radiance, and Maclean blinked blindly in the sudden glare. Ricky was standing by the doorway; to his right was a small trestle bed from which he had just risen. The gun in his right hand again forbade argument.

'You're about the dumbest dick I ever lamped,' he told Maclean. 'You surely weren't sap enough to think we'd leave this joint unguarded, with all that dope in the safe? Suppose some of the guys who're filed in there decided they didn't like paying up and wanted their letters or photographs back?'

'I guess I *am* dumb, at that,' Maclean agreed. 'Only I didn't know if you kept the stuff here or someplace else. Besides, I figured maybe you wouldn't be allowed to stay in this building all night.'

'We got special permission, pal,' Ricky said. 'But forget that. You know what's coming to you, don't you? I thought you were laying off the case.'

'Okay,' Maclean said, 'you got me. But how're you going to get rid of the body?'

'Easy. I'll simply clobber you over the head and drop you out the back window there, seventy-five feet down. Then I'll make sure you're dead. When they find you, they won't know where you came from.'

Ricky was so confident Maclean was yellow after what had happened a few hours before that he was careless. His gun hand was drooping slowly but surely until the muzzle was pointing on the ground just in front of Maclean. The detective's groping hands found the small tool kit behind him on the floor. It was heavy; there was a jemmy in there among other things. His fingers hooked around it.

'You're too nosey for your own good,' Ricky was saying. 'If I didn't bump you off, sooner or later someone else would.'

Maclean risked everything on his desperate throw at that moment. The tool kit whizzed across the room towards Ricky, and Maclean raced after it. Ricky's gun coughed, but the slug went wide of Maclean's flying body. Then the tool kit hit home, and Maclean right after it. Ricky cannoned against the wall and almost bounced off it, with his gun spitting lead. But Maclean was before him, and one shot tore home into the gangster just above his waistline. He went down with it, his gun clattering uselessly to one side.

Maclean bent over him and decided he wouldn't last long. Ricky was squirming and jumping like a slugged rabbit, and his eyes were protruding in the knowledge that he was fatally hit. Maclean picked up the hood's gun and went back to the safe. Seconds sufficed to open it; the combination was not intricate, and it wasn't the first time he'd done that sort of thing. There was a small file box, open, inside. Maclean thumbed through it down in the Gs. He was looking for Grant — Melanie Grant.

He didn't find any file on her at all. He hadn't really expected to — it was just a forlorn hope that Miss Nilo would have been methodical enough to file everything. Maclean had found out most women were like that. But if she had, the record wasn't there.

There was plenty of other stuff; enough to blow a third of New York's upper stratum out of their smug self-conceit. But it wasn't any use to Maclean. He emptied it all into a neat pile in the grate in front of the built-in electric fire, then touched a match to it. It flared up.

At least Miss Nilo wouldn't operate on those people again. Neither would Ricky; he had ceased twitching, and was dead. After ascertaining he was beyond help, Maclean left him there and went around wiping finger marks off everything. Then he left the office.

The night guard was still lying where he had fallen. Maclean skirted him carefully; he was glad he was still out. It would give him plenty of time to get away before Ricky's body was found. The cops would have roasted Maclean if he'd been implicated, hoodlum or not.

Dawn was sneaking over the scrapers, down into the canyon-like vastness of the city, when Maclean finally got home. And as he turned in to bed, glad to get some sleep after the stirring events of the night, Nose was half a mile away, staring down at all that remained of his partner.

10

Nose Knows What Goes!

Miss Nilo came downtown in a hurry, in answer to a harsh summons on the phone from Nose. The thug was waiting for her at the office.

'Siddown!' he snapped, jumping up as she came in. 'And shut the door!'

Frowning, she did as she was bade.

'Ricky's dead!' Nose rasped.

Nita Nilo gazed at him in astonishment. 'Dead . . . ?' she faltered.

'Yeah — an' he was *murdered*!' Nose was beside himself with rage. 'He'd been shot in the guts and left on the floor! I found his body when I came to relieve him!'

Miss Nilo gasped, glancing about her.

'He ain't here,' Nose grated, interpreting her action. 'I ain't stoopid! If his body had been found here, the cops would have been all over us and figured out our racket. I couldn't risk that!' He paused, his lips quivering. 'I got rid of his body. He's resting at the bottom of the Hudson.'

Miss Nilo expelled her breath in a long sigh of relief. 'How did you — ?'

'That don't matter now,' Nose snarled impatiently. 'What *does* matter is that we get the bastard who did for him — *Maclean*!'

Nita Nilo stiffened. 'Maclean?'

'Sure!' Nose's face was contorted with rage. 'It can't have been anyone else. This is what we get for lettin' him live — and it's *your* fault. You let the guy go free! You knew he'd pull something like this. Now we gotta do something about him. Now!'

'But . . . ' Miss Nilo frowned, prevaricating. 'He's got lots of friends who'd be sure call in the police. It's too risky.'

'We won't stick around!' Nose interrupted impatiently. 'I've got it all figured out. We can lam it to my brother Harry in Los Angeles. He'll look after us, and we can start up our racket there. Now, listen up — you're okay with Maclean. You phone him and ask him to meet you at your own place.'

'But you know I don't use my own flat for anything connected with — with the racket!'

'But this time you haveta. He bumped Ricky; we got to get him. Next it'll be me, then you.'

Miss Nilo looked worried. She knew if Nose got within ten yards of Maclean now, the lead would start flying; it was the only way Nose thought. She didn't want Maclean killed. More and more now, she didn't want it. More and more she hated the mess she'd gotten herself into, and wanted to get clear. But there was Nose glaring at her, beginning to wonder why she was making any objections now, after Maclean had killed Ricky.

Nose said: 'Well?'

'Let's take it calmly,' she told him. 'Don't rush into anything we can't handle. We don't want to attract the attention of the police.'

'They've been prowling around this morning. They were here just before you came in,' Nose told her. 'It seems Maclean slugged the janitor last night. They wanted to know if anything had been stolen from the office here. I told 'em no, but they're likely still in the building someplace. That's why we can't do anything right here. We haveta use your place.'

'But — how do you know he'll come?'

'He'll come for *you*. You phone him from your apartment and make out like you're in a jam. It's worth a try, ain't it?'

'No! We can't do it that way,' began Miss Nilo, and stopped as she saw the look on Nose's face. It wasn't a nice look; it actually made her shudder.

The light of homicidal mania was breaking through the clouds of obtuseness. Nose's trigger finger was itchy. And he didn't argue any more. He took her throat between his strong hands and began to squeeze. When her tongue protruded and her breathing came in harsh, tearing jerks, he loosened his grip and said: 'Call him — call him now. Tell him you found Ricky dead in your office this morning. Tell him you don't know what to do and you need help. Tell the sap anything, but get him to come over to your apartment! Hell, a guy who's just had ten thousand bucks outta you oughta do anything you say. Now get that phone!'

She got the phone; she was afraid of Nose, in this revolt of his. There was no telling what a man like him would do once his simple mind started revolving in a set circle.

But all the time she was on the phone, with Nose watching her for a false word, she was hoping Maclean would be astute enough to see that she was putting one over on him; that he would understand she had found the body, and was trying to get her hands on him. Under Nose's direction, she said when she contacted Maclean: 'Listen, Al — something terrible has happened. Ricky . . . he's dead. I found him in my office this morning. I want you to come over to my flat at once. You must help me, Al!'

'What kind of a gag is this?' came Maclean's tired tones.

'It isn't a gag,' she said, inspired by Nose's grip on her throat. 'I need you — need your help. You trusted me before!'

'Expect me in a half-hour. What's your address?'

She gave it him and thanked him, while in her mind she was calling him *fool, fool*!

She hung up and looked at Nose. His hands were twitching. He said: 'Let's get over to your dump, sister. Let's go!'

Maclean, meanwhile, was slipping into some clothing. He wasn't such a fool as Nita Nilo had assumed. Not Maclean. He had all his wits about him now, as he always had. He knew she must have suspected he had killed Ricky, and he was fully prepared to meet seven different kinds of trouble over at her apartment.

But he was going because he *liked* things that way, and if he didn't take a chance he'd never crack the case. She might be levelling with him, and really did need his help. He recalled his visit from Nose and Ricky, and how they had voiced their suspicions about her. Perhaps she was now afraid of Nose taking it out on her. And perhaps she would tell him what he needed to know to fit the missing links in the chain he had forged.

There was something else dragging him to her: was it the memory of that room at the Waldorf? Was it the memory of the invitation in her eyes? Or just the fact that she was bad, and that bad things exercised a fatal fascination for him? Perhaps it really would be fatal this time, he thought grimly as he slid into his necktie.

All the way across town in a cab, he told himself he was a fool to take this chance, and deserved all he got. Once or twice he turned his head to the speaking tube, as if he would instruct the driver to turn round and head back. But he never did, and at last he arrived at the entrance to the building in which Miss Nilo had her private apartments.

He paid the cabby off and stood looking at the place while minutes ticked by. He went in, got in the automatic elevator, pressed a button, and shot upwards. As he went, he snicked the safety catch of his gun off and made sure it was primed for rapid action.

He found the right number and played tunes on the bell. Miss Nilo called: 'Come in.'

He opened the door very cautiously and listened for a moment. Then he swung it wide, allowing his gaze to play around the room before he risked setting foot in it.

Miss Nilo was sitting on a tall-backed divan under the window. She was wearing a neat black dress that clung to her figure, with tan shoes and flesh-coloured stockings. The beauty of her almost made Maclean forget how dangerous she was.

She said: 'Come in, please, Al.'

'Are you alone?'

She nodded, but he hadn't missed the tautness of her voice, the strain and worry in her face, and the fear in her eyes. She said: 'Ricky was found dead at my office this morning. My files have been burned. Ricky was guarding them last night. He was shot through the side, just by the heart.'

'That's right. *I* shot him. It was him or me.'

'And you burned the files?'

'I did that too. I was looking for a file on Melanie Grant. There wasn't one.'

'There *is* one,' she said. 'Heaven knows

why I keep it, but there is.'

'It wasn't with the others.'

She shook her head. 'I'd hardly be fool enough to keep it there. It's a personal matter. If I had any sense, I'd burn it. I suppose it's the criminal ego in me that makes me keep it.'

Maclean didn't quite get her, but he said nothing more about it. 'You wanted my help?'

For the past few seconds her eyes had been hunting desperately around the room; now they focused on the door to the right and stayed glued there. She was trying to make him understand something, he could sense that. Was something behind that door?

He turned and went softly across the room. His foot lashed out, kicking open the door, and he jumped aside quickly. There was no movement. 'Come out of there,' he grunted, gun out in the open now.

No one came. But Nose's voice said: 'Throw your gun where I can see it, Maclean, and walk out into the open with your hands in the air. If you don't, I'll plug Miss Nilo — I've got her covered from here!'

Maclean swore and swung around. Nose was stood beside Miss Nilo, his gun poking in her ribs. Maclean cursed himself for a fool — Nose had been crouched behind the divan, waiting for his chance to emerge and get the drop on him.

Miss Nilo was white and trembling, but she shook her head violently and said: 'Let him shoot me, Al. He'll kill you if you do as he says!'

Nose grated: 'I'll give you three to drop that gun. One, two . . . '

Maclean reluctantly released his grip on the weapon, which thudded to the floor. Nose grinned savagely and swung his gun away from Miss Nilo, levelling it at Maclean.

Maclean saw that Miss Nilo was mouthing silent words, her face screwed up in tension. She was about to make some play! And he was ready for it.

Miss Nilo suddenly emitted a piercing scream, throwing the divan and herself backwards. Instinctively, Nose swung round to look at her. It was the chance

Maclean needed — and he took it. He swung his right foot savagely, kicking at Nose's extended gun hand. The gun flew out of his agonised fingers and across the room.

As Nose swung back to face Maclean, his chin presented a perfect target. The detective unleased a haymaker that crashed into his jaw. Nose buckled at the knees, and as he sagged Maclean followed up his advantage with a vicious chop to the back of his neck with the edge of his stiffened hand. The hood collapsed in a huddle on the floor, unconscious.

As Maclean scooped up the two dropped guns, Miss Nilo scrambled up from the floor where she had fallen and righted the divan. She looked apprehensively at Nose where he lay, unmoving,

'What — what will you do with him?'

Maclean shrugged. 'I think I can clinch things now. I'll turn in the details of your organisation to the cops. Nose and Maisie Fredericks'll be roped in. Nose'll probably get the chair for the Dempster job, and Maisie'll get charged as an accessory.'

'And *I'll* get the chair as well,' said

Nita. 'Oh, don't worry about me, Al. I'm sorry I ever got into this mess now. It was the usual case of starting small and getting big ideas. But please believe me, I'd never have countenanced murder but for hiring these two thugs — Antonio Rickcardo and Bill Bendix, otherwise known as Nose. It didn't seem to affect me when they killed someone. The reality of it didn't hit me. But after I met you and you said all those things to me, I began to hate myself, and nothing mattered much then — except that I knew how rotten I looked in your eyes, and I felt just as rotten. I pretended I didn't care when you told me what you thought of me, but every word was like a stab at my heart . . . I've changed now, but not soon enough to keep me from the chair. But I don't mind — as long as you don't hate me as much as you did.'

Maclean couldn't believe his eyes as tears trickled down her cheeks onto her dress. He went over to her, put a hand on her shoulder, sat down beside her on the divan, and said: 'Did you ever tell them to kill anyone?'

'No, never. When Maisie Fredericks phoned and said you'd gone to Forester's, I just told them to get to him and warn him not to say anything. They decided themselves to kill him. They killed the Dempster woman against my orders, too.'

Soddenly she was in his arms, pressing against him, sobbing her heart out on his chest. 'Oh, Al, I've been bad. I only realise now how bad I've been. But if I've done one good thing in my life, it's been loving you! And because I loved you, I've sentenced myself to the chair; and I don't care!'

For a moment his mouth met hers; a shiver coursed along his spine at the warmth of her lips.

Suddenly, the hitherto still figure of Nose came to life! Scrambling to his feet, he hurtled across the room and out of the door.

'Hell!' Maclean untangled himself from Nita's embrace and leapt to his feet. 'The rat's trying to get away!' He lurched towards the open doorway. 'Not if I can — '

'Stop!'

Maclean froze in the doorway as Nita's cry rang out. He turned in puzzlement. She came forward and caught hold of his arm. 'Don't risk it, Al . . . it's not worth the candle. You see, I know where he's going.'

Maclean listened as Nita swiftly explained how Nose had revealed his plans back at her office. 'Don't you see, Al? Things are too hot for him to stay here in New York. There's nowhere else for him to go but to his brother in Los Angeles.'

Maclean smiled grimly. 'I guess you're right at that. All I have to do is to tip off the cops, and there'll be a nice reception committee awaiting him when he gets there.'

'That's it,' Nita said quietly, More tears ran down her cheeks.

Maclean came to a sudden decision. 'Beat it,' he snapped. 'I'll hang on an hour before I tell the cops anything. You get out of town — but fast!'

11

Salato Steps in Again

Gail Grant paced nervously up and down her room, impatiently waiting for Maclean to return. He had gone out that morning in a hurry, and as yet he was not back. The hands on her clock showed the time to be after nine at night, and she was worried for him.

It seemed to her Maclean was always getting into scrapes. That morning she had noticed he had had a nasty purple bruise covering his right cheek and his nose. He did not mention the cause to her, and when she had asked he laughed and said he'd bumped it against something.

She suspected he had bumped it against the fist of one of the two men who had called on him late the previous night. Just after he had left her, she had heard thuds from his room, which was directly above her own. She had almost gone up; but when she opened the door to do so, she spotted the two men descending the stairs again, and she hesitated to intrude on Maclean then.

He hadn't mentioned how he was getting along in the search for her sister, but she knew he would tell her if he thought there was anything she ought to know. She wondered about the money in the bank, and how Maclean had found out about it, and why he had been appointed trustee, and who had appointed him! She wasn't quite as dumb as Maclean and Miss Nilo thought. She was perfectly well aware that there was something fishy about that money. She knew banks didn't go handing out large sums to comparative strangers, simply because they happen to be sisters of their missing depositors.

But she trusted Maclean, and knew he would do nothing against her interests. Her intuition vouched for him, and she herself counted him as her only friend in New York. Therefore, she took his statement about her newfound wealth without making things awkward for him to explain.

If Maclean kidded himself he had taken her in, it wouldn't do him any harm.

The worry grew in her mind as the clock hands crept further on. She had only known Maclean a few days, but he always seemed to be dashing off somewhere. Perhaps, one of these days, he wouldn't come back.

She drove the idea away and went downstairs. Good Time Rosie was in her rooms, and Gail knew she would be welcome. Good Time liked to hold forth on her conquests, and although she privately shocked the country woman, Gail saw that behind her bluntness and laxity she concealed a heart as big as the Empire State Building.

Rosie waved her to a handy chair and said: 'You look all het up, kiddo. What's wrong?'

'It's Al,' Gail told her. 'I — I can't make him out. He seems to — to act so funny.'

'Funny?'

'Yes — the way he dashes in and out.'

Rosie smiled. 'He's always like that when he's on a case. Maclean moves in

136

mysterious ways. He'll slack off soon, and if I were you I wouldn't worry overmuch about his comings and goings.'

'I — I can't help it. I — '

'You're stuck on him,' Rosie told her shrewdly. 'Isn't he a bit old for you, kid?'

'I — how old is he, Rosie?'

'Thirty-eight, maybe more.'

'Funny.' Gail smiled. 'That seemed awfully old to me before I met him. Now it seems hardly any age.'

'I know. That's the way love acts, kid.'

Gail flushed a little and tried to shake her head, as if to disclaim the imputation. But she couldn't resist saying: 'Is he — or has he ever been — married?'

'Maclean? No, not that I know of. I believe he did once love some woman — over in India, of all places! But she died.'

'Was he upset?'

'Was he? I'll say he was. He was in a mental home for long enough.'

'He must have loved her terribly,' said Gail wistfully.

'I don't think it was the extent of his love so much as the way she died — she died *for* him, you see, and in a nasty way. I don't quite know how, but I understand it was like that.'

'And there hasn't been anyone else?'

'No one.'

They sat in silence for a moment, then the telephone in the hall rang. Good Time got up to answer it. She came back and said: 'It's for you, dear. Urgent!'

Gail went out and picked up the phone. 'Hello?'

'Is that Gail?' asked a voice; it sounded hoarse and strained. Gail replied: 'Yes, this is Gail Grant. Who is that?'

'This is Mr. Maclean,' panted the voice, and Gail's heart jumped with anxiety. Seemingly something was wrong; it must be to make Maclean use those formal words to her when he had been listening to her calling him Al for the last two days.

'Al! What is it?'

'You're looking for a missing sister, aren't you?'

'You know I am. What . . . ?'

'She's here! Come as quickly as you can. She's dying. The address is fifty

Riverside Drive. It's an empty house, but I'll be there to let you in. Tell Good Time Rosie you've found your sister and are going to see her. Leave the address with her in case anyone calls.'

'But Al — '

'Don't argue if you want to see her alive! Get moving!'

Dazed with horror, Gail rushed back to Good Time and burst out: 'It was Al! He's found — found Melanie. I've got to go at once — she's dying. He said to leave my address with you — fifty Riverside Drive.'

Then without waiting for hat and coat, she ran out to find a cab. Her heart was thumping painfully, and she hardly noticed the evening chill through her light summer frock. Melanie — dying! Melanie, who had always been like a queen to her, who had always been with her until that day when Melanie had left home against their parents' wishes. And now — Maclean had found her and she was dying!

'Please go faster,' she cried to the driver.

'Lady, this is a taxicab, not an aeroplane!' was the laconic reply.

It was only minutes, but it seemed hours, before they were coursing along by the Hudson. The cabby pulled up outside a large deserted building standing in its own grounds. Hollow eyes of windows peered at her from the moon-ridden darkness, and the front door was like a huge maw which would open and swallow her up.

In a calmer moment, she would have paused and thought before knocking, or even walking up the steps. But with the panic-stricken idea that Melanie was dying without a friend or relation in that gloomy old mausoleum, she didn't even hesitate. Her fist hammered on the door as the cab rolled away.

The door opened, and from the darkness within a voice said: 'Come in, quickly — you're in time.'

Even then no warning bell rang; and it wasn't until she had stepped in, closing the door, and trying to penetrate the gloom, that she realised how strange it all was.

Then it was too late! Vice-like arms closed about her, and, kicking and struggling, she was borne away into the dark fastness of the empty house.

★   ★   ★

Maclean paid off his cab and entered the hotel. He had stopped on his way home for a leisurely meal, keeping his promise to Nita, to give her time to escape. He hoped she'd make it. Now, however, he would have to grasp the nettle and contact the police.

But he was fated not to make the call. He ran into Rosie as he was making for the stairs. She stared at him and said: 'How's Melanie? Have you left her?'

Maclean didn't get it. 'Melanie who?'

'Melanie Grant — you phoned and asked Gail to go to an address on Riverside.'

'I *what*?' Maclean grabbed her by the shoulders.

Rosie stammered: 'Hey. *Hey!* Take it easy. What's hit you? You phoned not two hours ago and asked Gail to dash over to

141

a Riverside Drive address — number fifty, she told me. You told her you'd found her sister, and that she was dying!'

'What was that address?' snapped Maclean, his face hard and grim.

Rosie told him again and stuttered: 'You don't mean to tell me you didn't — didn't phone?'

'I didn't! I don't know exactly what's going on, but if I don't get back with Gail in an hour, phone the cops and tell them to get down to that address you gave me!'

Then he had gone again, coat flying after him as he raced to grab a cab. It was the old Maclean, dashing head first into trouble without stopping to think it out. Had he threshed it out of Rosie a while longer, he would have learned that Gail had been *instructed* to leave the address she was going to. That would have told him it was a plant, and he wouldn't have been quite so reckless. But all he could think of was that someone had called Gail in his name, saying her sister was dying, and to get over. And Maclean knew that was a wild improbability.

Riverside Drive showed up, gaunt and

forbidding in the night. A blood-red moon lowered above the buildings, and in front the river swished unheedingly along towards the harbour. Maclean found number fifty and hopped out of the cab. He went up the steps in a rush and raised his hand to hammer on the door, then noticed it was open slightly.

Caution overtook him, and he fumbled in his pocket for his gun. With it gripped firmly in his hand, he pushed open the door and stared into pitch blackness. He took a step forward, so that he was outlined against the doorway. He heard the cough of a silenced gun, saw a tiny pin point of light roaring towards him, felt the slug strike his head, and knew he had landed head first into trouble.

He went down with his own gun blazing.

He was ploughing through a dismal, miasmic swamp, shrouded in darkness. Antediluvian creatures crawled nauseatingly over him as he strained onwards, onwards towards a glimmer of light in the distance.

He was wet with sweat, and foul odours

assailed his nostrils; giant carnivorous bats swooped silently above him, beating at him with rustling wings, trying to toss him back into the mire he had crawled from.

Faces grew in the dimness: Gail's face; Miss Nilo's face. Nose was there, gibbering at him wildly, and Ricky stared from the heart of the swamp with dead fish-like eyes. The enticing form of Maisie Fredericks tantalized him, but ever as he reached for it, it glided further back into those shadows away from that pinpoint of light.

Resolutely he turned his face against her and plodded on, the black knee-deep ooze clinging in masses to his legs as if it would drag him down, down into its depths.

Slowly that primeval wildness faded, and he was conscious only of that faint light which promised salvation and safety. Eagerly he beat his way towards it, and it grew brighter, brighter.

His head whirled giddily, and he was staring at a flickering candle standing on an upturned box in a bare, wood-rotted room. Blood was flowing down his face, pouring into his eyes. He shook his head, tried to move, and found he was securely bound. He was lying on the floor — and lying opposite to him, most of her clothing ripped from her white youth, was Gail Grant!

Her eyes were open, and she was staring at Maclean with grief and terror in her gaze. Maclean coughed weakly. 'Hiya, kid!'

'Oh, Al,' she whispered, tears trickling down her face. 'I — I thought he'd killed you!'

Then Maclean became aware of the other presence in the room. Salato, with an evil leer on his thin features, sat on the ledge of a boarded-up window. His hand — the one Maclean had injured by kicking — was bandaged, but the left hand held a revolver. As Maclean looked towards him, he made a sardonic bow.

'We meet again — your Waterloo, eh, Mister Maclean?' he sneered.

Maclean said: 'What's the idea?'

'I had meant to kill you when you came in,' Salato told him softly. 'However, I am just as pleased that I only stunned you. You will now be able to witness Miss Grant's degradation before you die.'

'You set this trap?'

'Guilty, Mr. Maclean. Rather clever, was it not? I knew all about the delightful Gail's missing sister. I found that you were looking for her. I was following when you went into an eating house tonight and ordered supper. Then, when I knew you would not stir for at least an hour, I put my scheme into operation. Had Miss Grant possessed a grain of common sense, she would have wondered why I insisted on her leaving the address she was coming to. The address, of course, was for your benefit.'

Maclean laughed. 'You didn't think I'd walk into a thing like this alone? The cops are right behind me!'

'I think *that* is a lie, Mr. Maclean. After our little bout with the guns, I watched closely to see if you were followed. You weren't!'

'Okay, if you don't believe me, just wait a while, that's all.'

Salato smiled. 'I regret that I am unable

to wait any longer. We have already been here for fifteen minutes. Now that you are with us once more, I think we can safely pick up where we left off that day in the hotel — can we not, my dear?' he said, with a leer at the shuddering woman. 'But this time, Mr. Maclean, there will be no interference from you!'

'You're nuts,' Maclean said. 'Within a half-hour the police will be here — and they'll get you, Salato!'

'Within a half-hour I will be gone. And there will be one dead detective, and a beautiful woman floating down the Hudson! There will be nothing to connect us.'

He moved across to Gail, as Maclean heaved upon his bonds. She shrank from his unholy caresses. Maclean cursed.

'This time, my dear, no one will interrupt,' Salato said . . . and the room door crashed wildly open!

12

The Payoff

The woman stood poised on the threshold, an ugly little thirty-two in her right hand. Here and there her eyes darted, taking in every detail of the scene. Maclean thought he had seen her before; she had fair hair, a little tousled-looking, and she was wearing a white raincoat.

Gail screamed: 'Melanie!'

After that there was dead silence; for seconds it was like a tableau. Salato half spun round, the gun still in his grip, staring with flaming eyes at the intruder; Gail, a glad light in her eyes, yet a terrible fear behind it; and Maclean, trying hard to make things connect and click in his mind. And the woman herself standing in the doorway menacingly, weighing the scene up.

Salato pressed the trigger of his gun as she pressed hers. The two shots blended together in a hideous crack, and the woman spun half round, buckled at the knees, and thumped down into a kneeling position. Gail screamed again — and fainted.

Salato drew another bead on the intruder; but before he could fire, her gun spoke again — once, twice, three times. Salato shrieked for the last time; her shooting was uncanny. Maclean was fascinated by the three neat holes in a row on Salato's forehead, as he keeled backwards to the floor. The woman dropped her revolver; her hand went to her side, and she opened her lips to speak, but no sound came. Her left hand dropped to the floor, bracing her body, and her lips broke into a painful smile. She started working her way across the floor towards Maclean — a hard, pain-wracked struggle for her. She reached him, and her hand went into his pocket, finding his jackknife. As she began to saw laboriously through his bonds, her dimming eyes met Maclean's.

She whispered: 'You — know — me?'

'I think I do,' said Maclean. 'I've suspected this ever since I noticed today that Miss Nilo had a *fair* parting in her black hair!'

'I — I had it dyed today, after you told me to get out of town. I thought that if I had the dye removed, I could come back again as Melanie Grant, say I'd been suffering from amnesia, and take up my life where I cut it off so long ago. I wanted to be with my kid sister, Al — and with . . . with you. I went back to the Rose Graham Hotel tonight — Rose told me what had happened. I got the address and followed. Lucky — lucky I did.'

His bonds were almost sawn through, but it was hard going for her. Blood welled from her wounds. She went on: 'I'm sorry I had to go out like this. But Al, don't — don't tell — the kid. Let her — let her think I'm okay. Don't tell her — what — what I'm really like.'

'I won't,' he said. Rapidly he was untying the rope from his legs. 'Whatever you did, you've more than atoned for.'

She was lying on her side now, blood welling from her wound. 'We could have — had fun, Al. Tell — tell the kid . . . Wake her up — I want to see her.'

Maclean went over to Gail, who began to stir as he started untying her bonds. He was only halfway through when a choking rattle made him hurry back to Melanie Grant, alias Miss Nilo.

She was dead, and his face showed it. And Gail read his face and burst into a flood of heartbroken tears.

★ ★ ★

Maclean found her car parked outside and managed to collect her case. It was packed with the usual feminine garments, and, on returning to the house, he passed it over to Gail — but not until he had taken out the small red book.

The book was what he had wanted. It was a diary of Melanie Grant's life — a five-year diary. It dated from before her disappearance to the present moment. Maclean remembered her words of that morning, when she said there *was* a file on Melanie Grant — a personal matter. He suspected it might be in her things, and he hadn't wanted Gail to find it. Gail believed Melanie had been out of town somewhere. She had no idea.

Suddenly there was a heavy bumping

below; the clump of many large feet on the stairs. Maclean smiled somewhat bitterly. The police had arrived!

He had a lot to tell them — and, remembering his promise to the dying Melanie, a lot *not* to tell them.

* * *

At first, the police had wanted to give Maclean a hard time. But the tearful testimony of Gail Grant — obviously blindingly truthful and sincere in her emotional extremity at the death of her long-lost sister — soon cleared him of all suspicion. And the slugs in Salato's body were swiftly established as having come from Melanie's gun. As the police interrogation proceeded, and the story of Maclean's earlier chivalry in rescuing Gail from Salato's clutches at the hotel, the detective in fact began to earn for himself a police commendation. Before he went to the hospital to have his wounds treated, hints even began to be dropped that his investigator's licence might be restored. And indeed, by the time he was released to convalesce back at his hotel, it was!

What had tipped the scales in his favour was an inspiration he had had when the police had asked him if the dead woman had passed any dying words to him before she'd expired. Any clue as to where she had been for five years, and why she had come back? The police sat up when Maclean told his story. Yes, she *had* whispered something to him. But, unfortunately, she had not had time to explain the mystery of her disappearance. All she had said was: 'Tell the police . . . the Dempster woman and Forester were murdered by Bill Bendix. And Bendix is being sheltered by his brother Harry in Los Angeles.'

No, Maclean had no idea what she had been talking about; but, he suggested brightly, maybe she had learned of these crimes — and maybe other, earlier crimes — and been in hiding for her life. And on learning that Nose had left for Los Angeles, maybe she had decided to come forward.

The police moved quickly on this information received, and Bill Bendix — alias Nose — was arrested on arrival.

Strangely, the baffled and nonplussed criminal never linked Maclean to his betrayal, and he went to the chair still mystified.

★　★　★

Maclean, confined to his bed with his wounds, was finally able to read the diary he had kept from both the police and Gail. He read it through, but the part he was really interested in began in March, 1943.

March 7, 1943.
Maisie is going to marry Fredericks for his money. I'm a fool to put up with this life when I can easily marry old Forester — he hasn't got any looks, but he has got money!

More followed some unimportant entries, then:

May 12, 1943.
I needn't marry Forester after all! Today I discovered he'd been playing the markets crookedly. I managed to

secure some letters from his desk — if they're published, he'll be ruined. I think five thousand dollars a month not too high a price.

May 20, 1943.

I told him today. At first he raved and cursed, and threatened me with the police. But I was firm, and at last he gave in! I'm rich! This is easy money, and I deserve it after all the mauling I've stood from him. I can give the job at the Golden Garter up. I might even be able to send Gail to a decent school. But I expect my father would object to me having anything to do with her, now.

June 10, 1943.

Maisie has been married for a month. She is moving in rather high society, and has found out a good deal about the rabble which they wouldn't like publicised. She knew about my blackmailing Forester, and thinks, with her supplying information and me doing the actual dirty work, that we could make a fortune from the rich fools she knows, who seem to think of little else but intrigue. I told her I would think about it.

June 13, 1943.

I've done it! I've contrived to vanish from New York — at least, as Melanie Grant. Whether they think I've committed suicide or not, I don't know. But they'll never suspect I'm a certain Miss Nilo! I hired two thugs who Maisie found for me. I don't like them, but one has to have protection . . . Already I have six victims. Forester is still paying. He, of course, knows I am Melanie Grant. But he daren't talk.

Maclean read on, marvelling at the way the lure of gold had acted on an innocent country woman. The diary went from bad to worse.

June, 1945.

Ricky and Nose have killed the Dempster woman. It seems she threatened to talk when they went to her to exhort money, and in their panic they killed her. Fools! She wouldn't have talked. But the boys are too impulsive.

Then it came right to Maclean:

I met him for the first time today. He's looking for Melanie Grant, and he has no idea he's spoken to her. I meant to have him killed, but I can't do it. Ricky and Nose wanted to know why not, and I made some silly excuse. I don't like the way they look at me now. But I'm seeing him again tonight, at the Waldorf!

Later:

He's just as honest and decent as I thought he would be. Oh God, why did I ever get into this mess? I'm really sorry — I didn't realise how rotten I was until he said those things to me. What can I do to get clear now?

It was the final entry in the diary; seemingly Melanie hadn't had time to record anything else. Maclean sat staring into the fire for a long time, the diary held limply in his hand. Then, with a sudden jerk, he spun the book across the room and watched it fall into the fire; watched the flames lick around it, destroying it to the last word.

'Lucky Rose's joint is old-fashioned,' he murmured to himself. 'If I didn't have an open fire to burn it, Gail might have found it lying around.' He lay back restfully, his eyes fixed on the ceiling. His thoughts were far away in the past, in a certain room at the Waldorf, with a certain slim, voluptuous goddess.

The door opened and Gail came in with an armful of magazines. She glanced at the smouldering diary, recognised it for what it was, and said: 'Hello! Been destroying the secrets of your murky past?'

Maclean smiled at her as she came over. He said: 'Get me a whisky, will you, kid?'

'No whisky for you. Doctor's orders! You can have a nice glass of milk, though.'

Maclean groaned dolorously. Gail sat on the bed by his side and gazed at him tenderly. 'Listen,' he said, 'I promised Melanie I'd look after you.'

She smiled faintly and ruffled his hair. 'But *I'm* looking after *you* now, Al. Don't you like it better that way?'

And because there was so much of her sister in her, and because Maclean hadn't had anyone to look after him for a long time, and also because he felt a whole lot younger with her, he said: 'Okay, honey, you win. And maybe, when I'm up and about again, I'll be able to look after *you* then!'

Arrest
Ace Lannigan!

1

Ace Shuffles the Deck

Ace Lannigan strolled casually into his editor's office, flopped into his editor's easiest chair, selected and lit one of his editor's expensive cigarettes, collected his feet, dumped them on his editor's desk, and heaved a heavy sigh.

His editor, Michael Woodson of the great London daily, the *Modern Gazette*, glared at him, outraged. 'Look here, Lannigan,' he growled. 'In America it may have been the thing to flop your hat and your feet on the editor's desk, scrounge his cigarettes and grab his best chair, but over here it's different. In England reporters must show respect for their editor; if not, out they go on their unwashed necks. Since you've been on the staff of the *Gazette*, you have absolutely undermined the normal office routine. You're a bad influence on the office boy: only this morning, instead of the usual 'Good morning, sir,' he had the impudence to say 'Hiya, boss!' This, Lannigan, is due to you and you alone. When I enquired yesterday as to the whereabouts of the fiction editor, my own secretary, otherwise a charming woman, informed me that he 'flew the coop' about eleven o'clock, from which, after some discussion, I gathered that he left the premises at that hour.

'I like you, Lannigan; you have supplied us with material that has considerably boosted the sales of this paper. All I ask you is to show a little more respect for those who, if not superior in brain power, are at least superior in position.' This was broad sarcasm, but it failed to register on Lannigan.

'Okay, Chief!' he said, and removed his size nines from the desk. 'The sub-ed said you wanted to see me. If it's news — shoot!'

'It won't be news to you,' said the editor. 'Take a look at this!' He flung a copy of the *Daily Globe*, the *Gazette's* most powerful rival, across. Ace studied it with a smile. It consisted of a two-column article with a half-page headline:

GENTLEMAN FROM AMERICA MAKES WHOOPEE.

Ace Lannigan, star American reporter, last night made an appearance at the Savoy Carlton Club. Before the evening was over, the above gentleman, who was, we regret to state, inebriated, insisted on mounting a table and rendering, to the delight of all present, two choruses of 'The Star-Spangled Banner'. We assume that this is Mr. Lannigan's method of looking for 'scoops' for the *Gazette*. After his unusual performance . . .

There was more in the same vein. Ace laughed. 'Those guys sure must be hard up for news, to print this stuff.'

The editor did not laugh. 'Look here, Ace,' he said, unbending a little, 'if you aren't careful, this will lead to a newspaper feud — and it isn't the thing in England. Cut out this carousing. If you must get stewed, at least get stewed where you won't be noticed.'

Ace grinned again. His was a simple creed. When he wasn't working, he got three sheets to the wind. When he wasn't drinking, he was sleeping: saving his energy, he said, for an emergency. But actually when not on an assignment, Ace was supremely lazy.

'I'll try, Chief! Was there anything else?'

His editor nodded. He knew that Ace was the finest reporter this side of heaven; he knew that Ace Lannigan fan clubs existed all over the United States, and that expressions like 'Lannigan's luck' and 'brave as a Lannigan' were in current use there.

'Yes! I've an assignment here that every reporter in the country would give his right arm to cover. I'm giving it to you. Not even going to ask you to give your little finger for it. Just a promise to steer clear of the drink.'

Ace looked reproachful. 'You should know by now that I always stay away from the booze when I'm on the job, Chief.'

'I do, but I'm making sure. Mind you, it's a tough assignment; but you can handle it, I'm certain.'

'Spill it!' said Ace briskly.

The editor fished a sheet of notepaper out from the litter on his desk. 'Lannigan,' he said, 'you obtained the evidence that sent Mike Rafferty to the chair and busted up his gang. You were aided by a gentleman named Ricky the Lip, who turned informer on his friends. The States were too hot for you then; you came over here to work for the *Gazette*. I suppose you know that Ace has been under constant police protection since you left the States; that attempts have been made repeatedly to put him on the spot?'

Ace nodded.

'Ricky the Lip landed in England this morning,' said the editor, 'and I want you to get a story from him. The *Gazette* is the only paper that knows of Ricky's arrival here. We want his life story, and we'll pay well for it.'

Ace rose and picked up his hat, balancing it precariously on the back of his fair hair.

'You don't know his address, Chief?'

'No; that's your job. Ricky has two

bodyguards with him, and one of them came and sold me this information about an hour ago. I had him trailed, but he managed to lose his shadow.'

Ace Lannigan helped himself to another cigarette, flicked a dust speck from his sleeve, smiled an angelic smile, and took his departure. He was well acquainted with the psychology of Ricky the Lip. When in danger, Ricky preferred to mingle with a crowd rather than shiver and shudder in solitude: like his principles, the Lip was yellow. Therefore, Ace commenced his search by enquiring at the biggest hotels. He did not pursue the obvious course of asking at the reception desks. With his usual foresight, he made his enquiries from the bell boys and porters. Had they carried any luggage in for a new client that morning; luggage bearing labels of American origin? At the Plaza Carlton he was unsuccessful. At the Major Hotel he found that a Hiram Walters had checked in that morning with his two nieces. The bell boy had seen the nieces and he assured Ace that they were beautiful. Ace laughed that one off. It could hardly be Ricky. Not by any means could Ricky's strong-arm men have been described as beautiful.

The hands of Big Ben registered nine p.m. before Ace found a likely steer. It was the doorman, attired like an admiral in the cast of an Astaire musical, who supplied the tip. 'Yes, sir,' he said. 'A little weasel-like man and two big ugly brutes arrived about 'alf ten.'

'Did one of the ugly guys go out again shortly after?'

''E did, sir. An' if you ask me, 'e were right gangster-like!'

Ace slipped a ten-shilling note in the man's palm.

'Thank you, my good man!' he said, and melted into the hotel vestibule.

As Ace entered the dining room, the first thing he bumped into was the Lip and his cohorts. 'Well, bless my sweet socks!' said Ace with a smile. 'Such a happy meeting. If it isn't my erstwhile friend, Ricky the Lip.'

The Lip, a wizened rat-like person in a loud checked suit, scowled, and his bodyguards pushed hastily in front of him.

'My my! If it isn't Lefty Grogan acting

as stooge! I don't know *you*, I am afraid,' said Ace, addressing the other guard, who seemed to lack a dividing line between hair and eyebrows, 'but I don't like your face.'

The man, thus addressed, bristled. 'Fresh guy, huh?'

'Lay off, Lannigan,' said Ricky. 'He's okay. Whadda ya want, Ace?'

Ace Lannigan elbowed the protesting guards aside and attached himself to the Lip's coat sleeve. 'I want a word in your ear, Ricky. My, that is a beautiful suit you're wearing. Where'd you get it — Petticoat Lane?'

Ricky, suspecting an insult behind the remark, scowled. 'Where's Petticoat Lane?'

'That's where the aristocracy get their glad rags,' said Ace seriously.

'Oh, yeah!' said Ricky. 'I guess I did get a suit or two there.'

'That's what I thought,' said Ace. 'Let's go up to your room.'

Ricky's room turned out to be a vast suite on the third floor. He took Ace into his bedroom and left the guards in the adjoining room. Ace settled himself gracefully on the bed and crossed his legs. He appropriated one of Ricky's cigarettes from an ornate box and inhaled a fragrant lungful.

Ricky paced uneasily up and down the room. 'How did you find me?'

Ace smiled. 'That will be my little secret, brother. Let's get down to whys and wherefores instead. Now, the rag I toil for is willing to pay you — '

'You're working for an English paper?'

'I am! You are looking upon the business brains of the *Modern Gazette*. As I said — I wish you wouldn't interrupt, Ricky . . . Where was I? Oh, yes. The rag I work for is willing to pay you for the story of your murky past. Why anyone should want to read about a past like yours, Ricky, is beyond me, but there you are. Of course, I could write about your past myself, but it would lack that personal fillip. It's easy dough, Ricky. How about it: do we get it or don't we?'

Ricky the Lip pursed them. Looking at his protuberant schnozzle made Ace wonder why he had not been nicknamed the Nose.

'It's this way, Ace,' he began. 'I got all the dough I can carry — I salted some for a rainy day when I was younger — an' any personal life story of mine would wise up those mobsters to where I'm hanging out. Nope! I guess I don't go for it, Ace. I got dough. I got protection an' a pardon, I got the whole of this little island to discover, an' I got my health an' — '

'I shouldn't say *strength*,' cautioned Ace, 'or you'd be fooling yourself, Ricky.'

Ricky crossed to the window and gazed out, and Ace made no offer to crawl off the bed. 'Sure!' said Ricky. 'I don't got to worry none now — '

They were the last words he ever spoke. As he leaned on the window ledge, there was a tinkle of breaking glass, and Ricky the Lip sank to the floor of the room with a gasping cough.

Ace Lannigan betrayed no panic. Swiftly he slipped off the bed and switched the lights off. The shot had apparently come from a dark window in the block opposite to the hotel.

Ace turned Ricky over. The bullet had gone between his eyes. The Lip was dead mutton. Ace crossed the room and walked casually into that occupied by the two guards, who were playing crap. They gazed at him curiously as he opened the outer door.

'By the way, boys,' said Ace carelessly, 'Ricky is sleeping the sleep of the unjust. I shouldn't disturb him for a while.'

The guards nodded and went on with their game. Ace breathed a sigh of relief. If they had been aware that Ricky was punctured, they would have asked awkward questions. There might even have been an argument, and that Ace did not want at present. Down in the vestibule he telephoned his paper and gave them another scoop. That done, he dialed house service and requested to be put through to the suite Ricky had occupied. One of the guards answered the phone. 'Whossat?'

'Is that Grogan of the courteous manner?' enquired Ace.

He heard a grunt, then: ''At's me!'

'Well I guess you boys had better start looking for another job. You'll find Ricky in his room with a lump of lead between the eyes. He sleeps for keeps!' There was a startled roar at the other end of the wire, and chuckling, Ace rang off.

He left the hotel quickly, after informing Scotland Yard of the killing. He had no wish to be detained just at that particular moment. But before he retired that night, Ace had done many things, including an interview with a sombre, dour police inspector. No, said Ace, he had no idea who was responsible for the murder. Yes, he would be available when required, and would sign a statement. The inspector censured Ace about his having left the murder scene, but reluctantly accepted Ace's explanation that he hadn't fancied trying to explain things to Ricky's two heavies.

He studied the note that had been awaiting his return. 'You're next, Lannigan!' it read.

He smoked a final cigarette and tumbled into bed with an easy mind.

'You're kiddin!' said Ace Lannigan into the darkness.

'But didn't you have a look at the building opposite?' asked the editor the following morning.

'Sure I did!' said Ace. 'I went there before calling in at Scotland Yard. It was a block of offices. The watchman swore nobody had passed the doors back or front, and I passed myself off as a flatfoot and got him to show me upstairs. There was a corridor with a window located opposite the hotel, and a door at the other end leading to a fire escape, which I ascertained had been used for a quick getaway. It was all beautifully simple. I thought the cops were going to grab me for it at first, but it turns out the shot was fired from a high-powered rifle, and there were plenty of witnesses to say that I hadn't been toting one. After all, you'd hardly manage to conceal a rifle in your vest pocket. Then I got this note I told you about.'

'What about that?' asked Woodson. 'Had you better have police protection?'

'Nuts!' said Ace briefly. 'Today I am going on a glorious binge. The women, Chief! They love me!'

It was as Ace had said: the women loved him. It would be unfair to say that Ace did not love the women — he did, no one more. Ace fascinated the ladies and they fascinated Ace; but as soon as he saw that well-known gleam in their eyes — the minute he heard the choir tuning up in the dim distance — he folded his tent like the Arabs, and as silently beat it for parts unknown. Such was life! As a matter of fact, he had already detected that gleam in the pure blue eyes of his latest acquisition, a pretty London waitress by name of Gloria Evans. Something told Ace that he should be closing his little romance with her, for her eyes already held a proprietary look: but try as he would, he could not bring himself to hurt those blue eyes; could not just write her off as another recruit to the ranks of the broken-hearted floozies he had strewn America with. They spent a great day together: Richmond Park and the flowers in bloom were not much in Ace's line, but he tried to appear as if he were enjoying himself, and strangely, he succeeded.

'Oh, Ace!' said Gloria. 'I read all about

you being with that horrible gangster when he was shot. Please *do* take care of yourself, dear, won't you?'

Ace grinned a sickly grin and nodded. 'I'm just shuffling the deck, honey. The big play comes later, and somebody's due to get a grand slam!'

The matter wasn't mentioned again. Gloria knew that Ace played with the breaks; he had told her often. Nothing would change that, and Gloria preferred him that way to not at all.

They dined at the Savoy, and it was after midnight when they parted. Unable to find a late taxi, Ace commenced to walk back to his flat.

He made it in just under ten minutes and was fumbling for his key on the step when the heavily wielded sandbag crashed on the nape of neck. Somewhere birds began to tweet, and Ace Lannigan passed from the land of the conscious.

2

Ace Takes a Trick

Ace woke up suffering from a nasty headache. He was used to nasty headaches, through constant association with those which were the aftermath of a night on the tiles; but this particular headache was superior both in quantity and quality to any Ace had yet experienced. Slowly returning consciousness brought to him the memory of being slugged on the neck by persons unknown. Apparently this was what had been indicated by the note he had received. The fun and games had commenced. Who, wondered Ace, could be hopeful of putting him in a wooden box, in England?

He had completely wiped out the Rafferty gang, to the last man, and he was certain that none of the other mobs would take the trouble to come over the big pond just to bump Ricky and himself.

He opened his eyes cautiously, and shut them almost immediately. One glance had sufficed to reveal that he was tied to a chair in the centre of a well-lighted room. Seated just to his right were four men playing cards.

'Hey!' one of them mumbled suddenly. 'That jerk opened his peepers then!'

Someone crossed over to Ace and gazed down at him. 'Seems to be still asleep, Charlie.'

'Stick a pin in him,' suggested the first speaker. 'He may be playing it dumb, seeing if he can pick up anything from the small talk.'

Ace decided that the pin idea did not merit his whole-hearted approval and he slowly flickered his eyelids.

'He's with us again,' said the man above him. 'Shall I give him the water?'

A blinding shower of cold water was suddenly pitched over his head and face. Ace gasped and blinked himself to full consciousness. 'Hello, boys,' he drawled nonchalantly.

'Sassy, ain't he?' said the one called Charlie.

'What's the idea?' asked Ace. 'If you boys were short of a bird to take a hand of cards, you shoulda let me know. I'd have moseyed along for a hand. No need to bring me by force.'

'You won't be so bright and breezy in a short time, old man,' observed one of the seated men.

Ace favoured him with a penetrating stare. 'Well, well, well!' he exclaimed. 'If it isn't the Dude himself. How's the white slave traffic, Dude?'

'None of your clever patter!' said the Dude.

'Of course,' continued Ace. 'You've shaved off that delightful little toothbrush you used to wear, and you've dispensed with the jolly old monocle, but that phoney accent of yours gives you away every time, old bean!'

'Can it!' growled Charlie, whom Ace did not know.

'I'd like to get at the idea behind these murder and kidnap stunts that you boys seem to be dabbling in,' Ace said. 'Who's running this outfit?'

None of the card players answered him.

'Oh, come on now. Let's not start being bashful, gentlemen.'

'You'll maybe find out soon,' grunted Charlie.

Ace saw that they were not to be drawn. He tested the rope which bound his wrists behind him. It was quite secure. All he could now do was wait, and he composed himself and relaxed.

Somewhere a clock chimed three.

The card game dragged on endlessly.

Four chimes this time. Ace shook his head to keep awake. The collars of his shirt and jacket were damp and clammy, where the water had saturated them. Right then, Ace would have given a great deal to have had some of that water for drinking purposes.

There was the sound of a car sweeping up the drive outside. 'This'll be it now.' Charlie left the room and could be heard negotiating the bolts on the door.

The others present slid the cards together and stowed them in a table drawer. Charlie returned, followed closely by the latest arrival, and Ace blinked in amazement. A slender, light-haired woman had entered the room, and Ace set her down immediately as class. What could a woman like that be doing among a bunch of hoodlums like these? he wondered. She crossed to his chair and gazed at him for long minutes.

'So *you* are the famous, or shall I say infamous, Lannigan?'

Ace grinned. 'That's me, sweetheart!'

Her gloved hand crashed into his smiling lips with the full force of her right arm. When it fell to her side again, Ace was still smiling mockingly.

'Dear me,' he said, 'Temper, my good woman, temper!'

'Has he given you much trouble?' The question was addressed to the four gangsters.

'Not a bit,' supplied Ace coyly. 'I've just sat here and been a nice, quiet boy all night.'

'I suppose you know who I am?' she asked Ace.

'Haven't the foggiest. But if you'll leave me your phone number, I'll — '

'I am Mrs. Michael Rafferty, Mr. Lannigan!'

If Ace was surprised, he failed to show it. 'And quite a dish,' he said in a bantering tone of voice. 'Say what you like about your ex-husband Mrs. R., but he certainly knew how to pick 'em. Personally I had no idea that Mike was one of the world's unfortunates. You certainly kept the marriage quiet — not that I blame you. Being hitched to a plug-ugly like Mike, you'd naturally *want* it kept dark. Hardly a thing to boast about.'

The widow of Mike Rafferty sneered slightly. 'You may jest to your heart's content, Mr. Lannigan.'

'Call me Ace,' he murmured bashfully.

'The jests you make tonight will be your last on earth. Undoubtedly before the night is out you will be in hell — I assume that's your ultimate destination.'

'I will remember you to Mike when I arrive, Mrs. Rafferty.' Ace had ceased to grin. 'You know, I wondered who had it in for me. I never gave a thought to the feminine sex at all. How is it that a woman like you got mixed in with these mugs? No, don't answer that one. I know it's got whiskers, I suppose you know the kind of birds you have recruited for your little plans of revenge? No? Well now, the guy over there is quite well known for his part in the white slave trade. The other one on his right, I recall, knocked a girl of thirteen down one night with his car, and while she was still screaming in agony criminally assaulted her, later throwing her body into a reservoir. Isn't that right, Harry? For heaven's sake man, don't blush.'

Harry moved unexpectedly to the chair, overturned it, and kicked the helpless Ace in the face. Charlie pulled him away and righted the chair.

'Thanks!' gasped Ace, spitting blood and teeth. 'Now that Harry has had his innocent bit of fun, I'd really like to know how you whipped this bunch of curs into shape, my dear.'

There was a surly growl from 'this bunch of curs', and they made a threatening movement toward Ace. Mrs. Rafferty motioned them back. 'We have wasted too much time,' she snapped. 'We must kill him at once and dispose of the body as the boss has ordered.'

Ace pricked up his ears. 'I thought *you* were at the head of this charming gang, my dear Widow Rafferty.'

'There is one above me,' she replied, 'who has reason to hate you more than I, even. I am the only one who can contact the boss. Our friends here have never seen their leader.'

'That's a cute little set-up, Mrs. ex-Rafferty,' said Ace, playing for time. 'Your husband dies and another guy takes over all his dough, his rackets, and his wife!' He had expected the last shot to get home, but the woman did not even change expression.

'You are welcome to your opinions, Ace Lannigan. If there is any little thing you wish before we take you for that well-known ride, I believe they allowed my husband a last request. I will allow you the same treatment.'

Ace considered the matter. His brain was working at top speed. He had been in some tight corners, but not like this. 'I'd like a cigarette and a glass of rye whisky,' he decided.

Mrs. Rafferty took a revolver from her bag and motioned to one of the gangsters. He untied one of the reporter's arms and poured out the requisite glass of whisky. Rafferty herself stuck the cigarette between his lips and lit it for him.

'Okay,' said Ace as she bent over him, 'let's go!'

With lightning-like precision, he flung the whisky in her face, and as she staggered back, grasped the revolver with his free hand. His eyes, suddenly bleak and cold, jerked to the Dude, whose hand was sliding to his hip pocket. The revolver spoke, and with a yelp of agony the Dude clutched his shattered hand.

'Not cricket, old thing!' remonstrated Ace softly. 'Get over in the corner with your hands up — all except you, my dear Mrs. R. You may untie my legs.'

The whisky-soaked gangstress bent to do his bidding. His legs were free, when from the corner of his eye Ace spotted her sudden grasp at the legs of the chair. Before she could topple the chair backwards, his foot had connected violently with her stomach. She gave a thin shriek and curled up in front of him, squirming in her efforts to breathe.

'I'm sorry,' said Ace, regretfully, 'but you will insist on playing rough.' He rose to his feet and swung the chair in front of him. One of his arms was still bound to it. He beckoned the now one-handed Dude over and indicated the ropes. 'Start untying, brother,' he said, 'or I'll present you with another hand to match the one that isn't!'

The Dude obeyed fumingly, plastering Ace's head with a picturesque medley of very un-dude-like curses.

'Well, I never!' tut-tutted Ace. 'Such language from an aristocrat!'

Once the three remaining gangsters made a move, but the barrel of Ace's automatic spelled death and they thought better of it. Finally Ace had rounded all five of the criminals, including Mrs. Rafferty, into the corner, and he backed cautiously towards the French windows. They opened to his touch and Ace backed out.

'I am going to stay out here for a while,' he informed them, 'while you meditate upon the hard way life has with the ungodly. I will, of course, shoot the first man or woman to move!' He vanished and the windows closed on him.

For a second there was silence.

Then — 'What the hell are we standing here for?' demanded Harry. 'We're letting him get away scot-free. Come on!'

He moved towards the door. There was a report, a crash of glass from the window, and Harry clutched his knee, stopped moving and sank to the floor. The French windows opened slightly.

'Sorry!' drawled Ace. 'Can't say I didn't warn you!'

No one else moved. A minute passed, and another. Then from the front of the house the five heard a car engine start up.

'The bastard's got the car!' moaned Harry, and the four who still had sound legs rushed frantically out of the windows and round the house, leaving the moaning Harry to his own devices. They were in time to see the tail-lights of the big car sweeping through the gates. Charlie wrenched a revolver from a shoulder holster and fired wildly after it.

A mocking laugh was their only reply; that and the roar of the car's exhaust. They retired indoors and made hasty preparations to find fresh headquarters. Within ten minutes the house was deserted.

3

King in Play

The elderly Duchess of Deemstown bore her age well despite the unkind ravages of sixty-odd years of self-indulgence. The society papers were wont to point out with unctuous pride that despite her sixty-odd years, she had never entered a cinema in her life, nor yet seen a moving picture, which remark elicited from the average man the observation that if she didn't get a move on it would be too late. Not that the duchess was old-fashioned — oh, dear no! Her ruling hobby was an obsession for cars — motorcars of any and every make. Any automobile that was in any manner out of the ordinary — that had some novelty built in to its body — was fair game for the duchess. She had a fleet of twenty such mechanical marvels at her country seat.

Therefore, when early one summer

morning (the time was actually eleven-thirty a.m., but that was early morning to the dear duchess) a young man sent in his card to her hotel suite — she loved hotels — she was intrigued when she read:

A. A. Phillips.
Representing: Nubilt Inc.
The car with a built-in bar.

She received him in the morning room. He was a tall, elegant young man, and his right hand was neatly bandaged. He was attired in correct morning suit complete with carnation. His English was faultless, and by the phrasing and intonation of his words, the duchess assumed he was a man of excellent birth, down on his luck. He delivered his sales talk at some, length, stressing the many advantageous gadgets which the Nubilt car incorporated, especially the ultra-modern cocktail bar that appeared at the press of a stud (for passengers only, naturally). Finally he informed her that the car was right outside, and he would be overjoyed if he might have the pleasure of taking her for a little ride or a test run. The duchess rightly pointed out that all this was a little irregular — that in the first place he should have approached her secretary; but so fascinated was she with the idea of serving cocktails to her friends while actually in transit that she readily agreed to take a run at once.

'Here it is — what! Rather!' said the young man as they left the hotel. The duchess scrutinized the big black car by the kerb.

'It doesn't *seem* very unusual,' she said.

'Ah! But wait till you get inside the jolly old chariot. Then you will get a shock!' said Mr. A. A. Phillips, whose name was no more Phillips than a Hotentot's is Claude Algernon.

She got inside, the chauffeur touching his cap to her, and the bogus Mr. Phillips piled in after her. The car drove away. That was the last anyone saw or heard of the dear duchess for two days. Then, since there had been no accidents, it was assumed she had been kidnapped; and Scotland Yard fumed at the consummate ease with which this had been accomplished. It was rapidly established that although there was a Nubilt Inc., their firm was located in America: they had neither representatives nor cars in England.

Ace Lannigan read all this in bed. He had wired to the *New York Recorder*, giving a brief account of his abduction two weeks previously, and a description of the two members of the gang with whom he was unacquainted.

The *Recorder*, his old paper, had come through with the photographs and records of a number of lesser-known racketeers, and Ace found amongst them the men he sought. One was Charles Edwin Gubbins, a notorious (in a small way) fire bug; the other was an ex-bootlegger and kidnapper by the name of Pudge Martin, alias James Little.

Ace had had a quiet life for the last two weeks; his greatest exertions had been trying to trace the owner of the car he had commandeered from his enemies. He had been unsuccessful. The police had raided the house at which he had been held prisoner but had found nothing — the birds had flown.

He wondered idly why the charming Mrs. Rafferty had picked the men she had. Ace was well aware that the average crook has his own particular line and that nothing would persuade him to branch out into a different profession. For instance, the cracksman would no more think of becoming a bootlegger than the bootlegger would become a kidnapper or that worthy a killer. Cold-blooded killers were scarce. Most murders, Ace knew, were committed in the sudden fury of the moment. In all his long career as crime reporter for the *Recorder*, the cold-blooded murderers Ace had come across could be counted on the fingers of one hand, excluding the thumb.

Harry Benham, he whom Ace had shot in the leg, was one of these cold-blooded killers. Then there was Pudge Martin, a despised kidnapper; Charlie, an arson merchant; Dude Hays, white slave traffic and confidence trickster; and Mrs. Rafferty herself. What was she? Was she just out to avenge her husband, or was she also making a handsome profit from the doings of the gang? And who was the boss?

It was at this point that Ace read the account of the kidnapping of the Duchess of Deemstown; here was the answer! Obviously the salesman had been the Dude with his bandaged hand and his collection of other peoples' business cards; the driver most likely would have been Pudge, the experienced snatch man. Kidnapping extraordinary!

Very clever, mused Ace. He yawned, stretched, and lit his after-breakfast cigarette. At last he could start on the case again; the editor had given him carte blanche on the assignment. The gang had to be broken up, and if Ace accomplished it the publicity for the paper would be tremendous.

His reverie was shattered by a ring at the bell of the flat. Mrs. Hobson, the landlady, made an appearance in answer to Ace's 'come in.'

'There's a — a — gentleman to see you, sir,' she announced.

'Do I know any?' said Ace reflectively. 'Show him in, Mrs. H.'

The 'gentleman' turned out to be none other than one of Ricky's late bodyguards

— not Grogan, but the specimen with the unsorted hair and eyebrows. 'I'm Joey King!' he said self-consciously.

'I'm President Roosevelt,' said Ace. 'Have a chair.'

Joey sat on the edge of a chair, seemingly embarrassed, twiddling his Derby hat between agitated fingers.

'Have a cigarette?' suggested Ace.

'Naw, thanks.'

'A spot of toast and marmalade, or grapefruit? Coffee?'

'Guess not.'

'I love these intelligent conversations,' reflected Ace. 'So enlightening.'

The bodyguard twirled his hat, dropped it, scooped it up, stuck it unthinkingly on his bullet head, blushed scarlet, grabbed it off again too hastily, and caused it to go spinning across the room. He eyed it uneasily and stretched to reach it.

'Never mind the hat,' said Ace. 'What are you trying to sell me? A juggling act?'

'I was plenty fond of Ricky,' observed Mr. King.

'Well, there's no accounting for taste.'

'Yessir, plenty fond!'

'So you said.'

'I'm telling you — plenty.'

'Not again,' begged Ace.

Joey King reached out a cautious foot and drew in his hat. He replaced it on his knee. With the hat re-installed, he appeared to regain his self-possession. 'Mr. Lannigrass, I want — '

'Lannigan,' said Ace.

'Eh?'

'Never mind,' said Ace wearily. 'What was it you wanted?'

'A job, Mr. Lannigan!' He shot it out like a bullet, blushing a deep scarlet.

Ace betrayed no surprise. 'You do? What has all this to do with your fondness for Ricky and your ability to juggle your hat?'

'I read in the noospapers that you aim to bust open the mob of rats that put Ricky six feet under.'

'Right you are.'

'Okay, I wanta help you. I can tote a rod for you, Mr. Lannigan. I ain't afraid of those mugs. I got ants in my pants to get after 'em. How about it, Mr. Lannigan?'

197

Ace studied him intently. Certainly he needed an assistant, and Mr. King seemed to be sincere enough. 'What made you so fond of Ricky?' he asked.

Mr. King twiddled his hat furiously. 'He was my brudder!' he said. 'My real name's Joey Riccoli.'

Ace was accustomed to making rapid decisions. 'Okay Joey, you're in. By the way, what happened to Grogan?'

Joey heaved a sigh of satisfaction. 'He went back to the States.'

So it came about that at three o'clock that afternoon, a queerly paired couple made their way to the hotel. Majestique. They announced their desire to speak to the Duchess of Deemstown's private secretary, and were shown up to a sumptuous suite and told to wait.

'The ole dame coitainly does herself proud,' observed Mr. King, glancing about. 'What in hell's dis?'

'Dis' was a statuette of futuristic design, an irregular mass of womanly curves and hard angles, squares and triangles. Mr. King viewed it with unenlightened eyes. It bore a brief inscription on the feet of what was obviously meant to be a nude woman — 'The Unhappy Virgin'.

'De Unhappy Voigin,' read out Joey in puzzled tones. 'Why is de dame unhappy, boss?'

'She's a virgin,' said Ace gravely.

The light of understanding dawned in Joey's eyes. 'I swow! Dat accounts for de skoit bein' unhappy, I guess.'

A gentle cough caused Joey to replace the statuette as if it had been red hot. A young woman had entered the room and was gazing at Mr. King with obvious amusement. 'Good morning, gentlemen,' she said. 'I am the duchess's personal secretary.'

Ace rose from his seat and captured her eyes with his own. 'First of all, Miss — ?'

'Daly. Elsa Daly,' she replied.

'Miss Daly, first of all I want you to realise that I am only working in the interests of the duchess. You are in a position to assist me, Miss Daly.'

'Might I enquire who you are?'

'Of course. I am Lannigan of the *Gazette*, and this is my, er, personal, um, secretary, Mr. King.'

'How's tricks, sister,' supplemented Joey, looking about as much like a secretary as an Irish cop.

Miss Daly smiled. 'I've heard and read of you, Mr. Lannigan. How can I help you?'

'You can show me the ransom demand note that the kidnappers sent to you.'

It was one of those wild guesses that had brought home the goods for Ace before. He saw the quick tremor of the woman's eye.

'Note? Mr. Lannigan, I don't un — '

Ace sighed wearily. 'Please, Elsa!' He used her first name with impudent indifference, but the insolence was destroyed by the soft, reproachful smile he bestowed on her. 'Please don't say 'I don't understand.' Try to think of a new line.'

She smiled in return and watched him closely for a second or so. 'Very well — Ace!' she retorted, and he grinned. 'I did receive such a note.'

She fished a letter from her sleeve. Ace took it and read. It seemed to have originated from the old lady herself and was brief and to the point, informing Elsa to seal twenty thousand pounds in a plain envelope and send it by messenger to a small village near Kingston. On no account was she to inform anyone else of the arrangements, for to do so would imperil her mistress's life. The go-between would be met at the specified point by a man who would relieve him of the envelope. This done, the duchess would be released immediately. The appointed time for the ransom to be paid was twelve midnight, and the note pointed out that the bearer of the money must be alone.

A slow smile spread over Ace's face and he settled himself comfortably in an armchair, lit a cigarette, and proceeded to outline his plan. It involved the assistance of Mr. King, and that worthy was heart and soul for it. Miss Daly was a little dubious, but finally she, too, agreed.

The ransom was to be paid that very night, and shortly before nine p.m. Ace Lannigan took up his place of concealment behind some shrubs near the meeting place specified in the note and settled down for a long three-hour wait.

At a quarter to twelve, a lone figure was seen plodding cautiously along the road. He stopped at the meeting place and took concealment behind a tree after first making a rough examination of the cover in the vicinity. During this search, Ace had retreated to a prudent distance. When the search was over, flat on his stomach, he edged back to his vantage point.

At twelve p.m. precisely, another stocky figure appeared on the scene. It was Joey King, and in his hand he held the envelope plus the £20,000.

4

Ace High!

Joey King halted in the shadow of some trees, lit a cigar and waited. Ten minutes elapsed, and then from behind him came a soft whisper.

'Are you the messenger?'

Joey gave a start. 'Yup!' he said.

'Lay the money on the ground in front of you and raise your hands above your head. I've got a bead on you! Don't turn.'

'Say, how do we know you'll let the old judy go — ?'

'Do as I say!' snapped the voice a little louder. Joey did.

From his hiding place in the shrub, Ace saw a dark shadow steal up behind Joey; he heard a nasty thump and Joey sank to the earth. The shadowy figure chuckled and stooped for the money, slipping his gun in his pocket. At the same time, Ace, attired in rubber-soled pumps, moved. As the kidnapper straightened up he saw Ace a few feet away.

'Okay, Harry,' warned the reporter. 'Take it easy. I've got the bead on *you* this time.'

Harry Benham cursed roundly. Patiently Ace waited for him to finish. The flow of epithets finished abruptly.

'Turn around with your hands up, Benham.'

Harry did so, and quickly reversing the revolver, Ace caught him neatly on the base of the skull. Without a groan he sank beside Joey. Ace Lannigan sat with his back against the tree, lit up, and waited for Joey to come round. Once Benham appeared to be regaining his senses, Ace tapped him gently on the skull again.

While he sat, he introspected. Ace was philosophical. He realised that it was no use chaffing at the bonds, literally speaking. If it was necessary to wait, wait he would, patiently. The time by his wristwatch was twelve-twenty. Sitting there, he almost went to sleep. When Joey recovered it was one-fifty, and the roadway was littered with cigarette stubs.

As Joey sat up, Ace told him to be quiet a while and rest his head. Finally Ace picked up Benham as if he had weighed a couple of pounds, hoisted him on one shoulder and carried him beyond the shade of the trees.

Harry Benham woke up with a vivid sense of fear. He was in the hands of Ace Lannigan, and the stories he had heard about that noted gentleman's method of dealing with the unlawful were extremely unlawful. He shivered and gazed about him. Sitting on his right was the man from whom he had obtained the ransom money. On his left was that fair-haired giant Lannigan. His revolver had been removed from his pocket. The kneecap Ace had shattered two weeks ago was bent painfully beneath him. He straightened his leg, wincing.

'Hello, Harry,' said Ace conversationally. 'With us again, I see.'

Harry shuddered. 'What are you going to do with me?'

Ace considered. 'We want a little, information, Harry. First, where are your headquarters? And second, who is the boss?'

Benham made no reply.

'I fancied you wouldn't talk, Harry. Still, I think we can make you. I warn you, however, that I will have no scruples with regard to your injured leg. Any man who could get away with only three years in the pen after what you did to that girl deserves a little extra punishment. I consider myself quite qualified to administer it.'

'You'll be sorry if you touch me, Lannigan!'

Ace smiled tolerantly. 'That one is so old it doesn't even rate a laugh, Harry boy.'

Joey took hold of Benham's arms and held them in a lock behind that unfortunate. Ace broke a slender branch from a tree. It was about two inches thick and two feet long. He swished it appraisingly.

'You aren't going to use that on my back?' quavered Harry.

'Worse than that, Harry lad! Just tell us where the old lady is.'

A stubborn tightening of the lips was his only answer. Selecting his place with great care, Ace bestowed a terrific blow on the gunman's already wounded kneecap. Harry Benham shrieked out in savage agony.

'Dear me!' said Ace. 'What a terrible noise he does make. Don't be a baby, Harry, boy. Keep a stiff upper lip.'

Harry knew quite well that his screams would not be heard. He himself had chosen this spot for its utter loneliness. He cursed and refused to give any information. Ace wasted no more time. The stick rose and fell on Harry's tortured limb with monotonous regularity. With a vision of the agonised woman Harry had once shown no mercy to, he hit with a will. Harry screamed and cursed, shrieked and moaned, his legs thrashing up the ground he lay on; but there was no mercy for him. At last through foam- and blood-flecked lips he told all he knew.

'They got the old dame at a house in Kingston,' he babbled. 'If I ain't back by six o'clock this morning, they'll kill her and make a getaway.'

'Who is the boss?'

'I don't know,' sobbed Harry. 'None of us know except Rafferty's wife. All I know is that the two of them are connected with some kinda night club in London.'

'How did they come to get hold of you boys in the first place?' asked Ace. 'Why didn't they compose the gang of real mobsters like you? Where does the Dude come into this, and how about the fire-bug?'

'We were all down on our luck,' groaned Harry. 'She contacted us as soon as we left the prison. All of us had just done long stretches and were having a tough time making a fresh start. The busies were watching us like a bunch of Brooklyn boys watching the Dodgers play ball. This Rafferty dame suggests that we cross to England and make a fresh start. She pays the passage, and in return we help her and the person above her to rub out you and Ricky. When that's done, she says she'll set us up in our own rackets over this side and call on us when there's any big jobs on.'

'You don't know the name of this night club you say the boss is mixed up in?'

'I don't know nothin' else,' whined Harry.

Ace handed the stick to Joey. 'Okay, Joey — I think you wanta ask him a thing or two, don't you?'

'Sure,' said Joey grimly. 'Just one little t'ing. Who shot Ricky?'

'I don't know,' said Harry, squirming in anticipation.

Joey raised the stick.

'I tell you I don't know!' howled Benham in terror. 'All I know is that when Ricky was shot, me and the Dude and the dame was all together arranging this kidnapping, an' Martin and the other guy was delivering that warning to Lannigan's apartment. If it was anyone outa the mob, it musta been the boss.'

Ace studied his watch. 'Four o'clock! Okay, Suppose you take this yellow-bellied whatsit to the car you came in, Joey.'

Joey picked the suffering gangster up and the trio proceeded along the lane. Ace's car was parked on the corner and Harry was firmly bound and dumped into the rear seat. Joey sat with him just in case. Ace said: 'He's frightened of the dark.' Following directions issued by

Benham from the rear seat, the car proceeded on its mission. The outskirts of Kingston flashed past, then the town itself. They were about half a mile past Kingston when Harry gave them to understand that they were near their destination. Ace applied the brakes, cut the lights, and with Joey carrying Harry, they left the car again.

The hapless Harry led them to a large rambling mansion. The dawn was breaking as they drew near to the drive; and Harry, when questioned, said that it had not been thought necessary to post a guard at the gate. Merging with the shadowy oaks and yews along the drive, they trod carefully towards the house. Harry, having brought them this far, decided he might as well turn traitor altogether. He produced his own key, and with it, Ace opened the front door. The three passed into the hall and stood silently. The house was wrapped in gloom; not a sound or light on the ground floor. Harry had taken a violent fit of shivering. He was thinking of the probable fate that his accomplices would mete out to him if ever they got hold of him again. The underworld has a short way with stool pigeons.

'Where have they put the old lady?' asked Ace in a whisper.

'On the second floor,' said Harry hoarsely. 'In a back room.'

Ace fumbled against a telephone on a small table. Silently he lifted the receiver and requested Emergency. 'Put me on to the nearest police station to Kingston!' He waited a moment. 'Hello? Good. Send a squad of men over to — ' He paused and obtained the address from Harry. ' — to Manor Lodge, on the outskirts of Kingston, immediately. The gang that kidnapped the duchess are over here. What? All right, then phone the Yard! Tell them this is Ace Lannigan of the *Gazette*, and tell them to jerk it up some!' He slammed the receiver down again. He motioned his companions to go up the stairs, and silently opened the door and left it ajar. Then, slipping a revolver from his pocket, he followed. They gained the first landing in silence, and became aware of voices. They came from a room at the end of the passage.

'That's the room they got the old woman in!' whispered Harry. They crept closer to the door.

'Look here,' said Charles Edwin Gubbins peevishly, 'I reckon Harry's been gone plenty long enough. I don't like it. Whose bright idea was it for him not to go in a car?'

'The boss arranged everything!' snapped the Dude, crossing his elegant legs. 'If Benham had taken the car and something had gone wrong, how would we have made our getaway? Stop crowing, old top! Dash it all, it's a deuced long trot from here to there. What? He should be back any time now.'

The Duchess of Deemstown, tied to a chair in one corner, was still wide-eyed with wonder. 'Are you gentlemen *really* American gangsters?' she asked.

'Whadda you think, Ma?' retorted Pudge Martin.

'What an experience to tell my friends about!' said the duchess, who, apart from the slight discomfort of being bound, was too obtuse to appreciate the real danger she was in.

'If you live to see your friends again, my dear Duchess!' said the Dude.

'Now you are joking,' said the 'dear duchess'.

'Pipe down, Ma, before I bop you!' snarled the Dude with a complete reversal of form.

'Ma' piped down.

'What's the time?' asked Charlie.

The Dude studied his elegant wrist-watch. It was four-thirty. 'He should be back by now,' he said thoughtfully, 'unless there was a slip-up. Now you mention it, the arrangements for this stunt weren't all they should have been. I notice that our charming second-in-command has not put in an appearance tonight. Too risky for her, most likely. I don't like the way she's acting either. Seems to have dropped out of the game lately. I think we'll have to look out for — ' The door shot open and Ace gazed mockingly in from the rear of his wicked-looking revolver.

'Don't bother, pal!' he remarked. 'I'll look out for *you* instead. Quite the happy party here, aren't you? Where's the delightful widow Rafferty? We only need her and we'll all be set for another Phil the Fluter's Ball.'

To say that the occupants of that room were perturbed would be understating the case. Every gangster in the States had a healthy respect for Ace Lannigan. When he took up the trail he kept to it, and his luck was usually excellent.

The frightened eyes of Dude Hays followed Ace and his revolver as they edged into the room. Ace poised himself lightly on the table's edge.

'Come in, Joey! You too, Harry. The boys'll be no end bucked to see you! They were just worrying about you. Come in! Set their cheery little hearts at rest.'

Joey King, with Harry hanging unwillingly on his shoulder, entered. Harry glanced at his companions in crime with narrowed, fear-filled eyes. Joey sat him down in a convenient chair.

'You little bastard!' hissed Charlie at him. This merited a shocked glance from the Duchess of Deemstown. Harry said nothing. Deprived of a gun, he was an arrant coward.

'Isn't he?' observed Ace. 'And you are a

bigger one, Edwin!'

Charles Edwin Gubbins fixed Ace with a cold eye. 'You think you're pretty slick, Lannigan,' he rasped. 'You're lucky, I guess, but it won't hold out forever. One of these days someone'll fill you so fulla lead that they'll be able to use you for a cheese grater.'

Lannigan was amused. 'Very witty, Edwin,' he said. 'But don't you think you'd better cut the small talk? And while you're at it, cut those ropes that are incommoding the poor duchess. I'm sure she must be fearfully bored with your company.'

Ace was prepared for the next event. The look in the gangster's eyes had not escaped him. Charlie bent over the duchess and fumbled. The duchess screamed a warning as she divined his intention; then Charlie had whirled around holding a revolver snatched from his shoulder holster. He fired two shots as he turned, one at Harry and one at Ace. Harry suddenly rose to his feet, clutched convulsively at his head and dropped.

The bullet intended for Ace missed; for

even as Charlie fired, Ace was sliding to the floor, firing as he fell. His aim was unerring. Charlie had no second chance to shoot. The revolver dropped from his nerveless fingers, and he slumped to the floor with a bullet clean through the eye and into the brain. Ace picked himself up in time to see the door close behind the Dude and Pudge Martin. The key turned on the outside.

Joey, heaven bless him, had been too slow to prevent the escape. He was gazing with popping optics at the two new corpses. He now turned and applied a hefty shoulder to the door. It was solid oak and he merely succeeded in twisting a ligament, which wrung from him a curse of annoyance. Ace fired a couple of shots into the lock, but before it gave they heard the sound of the mobsters' car tearing down the drive. It had hardly died in the distance when a couple of cars tore up the path.

'The minions of the law,' observed Ace. 'Too late — as usual.'

5

Knockout Whilst in Clubs

His newspaper provided Ace with legal representation, and his lawyer, aided by the valuable testimony of the duchess, was able to establish a sef-defence plea for the demise of Charlie.

Ace Lannigan was not, in the normal course, unduly vicious or brutal. But he was prone to react according to type of person he was dealing with. With mobsters such as Harry Benham, one could not merely scold them. In dealing with callousness, Ace was himself callous. He had a reputation among American thugs of shooting to kill if his own life was jeopardised. And it could be argued that the punishment he meted out to Benham was richly deserved. Ace was no conventional hero — no clean-limbed, god-fearing man; for Ace owned no god save one of his own making: the great god Adventure.

Such would have been apparent from a glance from the litter of odds and ends that were strewn about his flat. Here a crime story magazine: Ace loved to read them in spite of the fact that he was continually *living* a crime story more unbelievable than any he had read; there a neat revolver, stripped ready for cleaning. A copy of the New York *Police Gazette*; a copy of *La Vie Parisienne*; a short bowie knife and a bottle of chloroform — in fact, a hundred things you would not find in the average English home: these things were the essence of Ace Lannigan; the little things he delighted in.

Three days after the rescue of the duchess, he rolled home to his flat with Joey King in an inebriated condition. The two had been going the rounds of the London night clubs, bearing in mind what Harry Benham had told them. As they entered Ace's flat, his landlady, Mrs. Hobson, spotted him.

'Oh, Mr. Lannigan!' she called. 'The man came to fix your shower!'

'What's that, Mrs. H.?' he asked, halting abruptly.

'The man you sent for to fix your shower, sir — he came while you was out this afternoon. He said you phoned this morning.'

'Oh, yes!' said Ace. 'Thash' right. Thanks, Mrs. H.'

They settled down on the sofa with a whisky and soda each. Ace wrinkled his nose and sniffed. He couldn't have sworn in his irresponsible condition, but he seemed to catch an acrid odour.

'I'm goin' to have shower!' he announced gravely. 'Clear my head!' He lurched to the bathroom and drew the curtains of the shower. He didn't bother to remove his clothes. Trifles like that never worried Ace after a successful binge. His hand was on the tap when he paused and stood as if transfixed.

Under his feet on the white tiles were several brown spots — discoloured patches of tile about a quarter-inch in diameter. Ace collected his medicine chest and made a brief test. He then returned to the living room, took a piece of cord and Mr. King, and walked quite steadily back to the shower. He attached the cord to one spoke of the tap, stood a safe distance away, and pulled. The shower operated for about one minute, then stopped.

'Wassamarrer?' demanded Joey. 'Whassa wader stopped rumiin' for?'

'It's stopped running,' Ace told him, sobered by the nearness of his peril, 'because the inlet pipe is blocked; and it was not, as you assume, water.'

'No?'

'No! It was a gentle little tonic known as, I think, sulphuric acid. Probably had I been under it, I would be blind by now. Vitriol in the eyes is hardly a pleasant thing. I knew there was something wrong around here. I never sent for anyone to fix the shower since it has always worked perfectly; and then there was that peculiarly pungent smell. Lucky I noticed the discolouration from those drops. And here— ' Ace had obtained a chair and climbed up to the tank above the shower. ' —is the glass carboy the acid was brought in. A gallon container. Quite a diabolical little stunt if it had come off. As I thought, the inlet pipe has been blocked and the water already in the tank must have been drained off. Very original!'

Mr. King was a little fuddled. He seized his suffering hat and twirled it about his fingers with much agitation. 'Who done it, boss?'

'It can only have been a member of the bunch we are already up against,' said Ace. 'However, let's get some sleep. I'll have this mess cleaned up in the morning.'

He indicated the shower curtain. The waterproof was burnt through and eaten away where the drips from the vitriolic acid had caught it.

★   ★   ★

'How many clubs,' said Ace, pouring himself another cup of coffee and ruefully surveying the portion of cremated bacon the good Mrs. Hobson had brought him, 'have we investigated so far?'

'Lessee!' said Joey thoughtfully. 'Dere was de Golden Shoe, where we had dem Silver Ladies; de Unicorn, where we drank dose Vampires — geeze!' said Mr. King reminiscently. 'Dem was soitanly de cat's eyebrows. Me head was near to coming offa me neck. Den dere was de Sound of Reveille by Night — '

'Sound of *revelry* by Night,' corrected Ace.

'Dat's what I sez. De Sound of Reveille by Night!'

Ace produced his notebook and studied it. 'Thirty-one!' he announced. 'Thirty-one in three days. Added to which, we have come home each of those three nights stinko.'

'Yeah! Who's doin' de payin' for de drinkin'?'

'I'll put that into the paper's hands. Comes under expenses.'

'Dere's a noo club I saw de odder day, boss. Called de Silver Garter.'

'Okay — we'll start there tonight, my fine feathered friend.'

Ace dropped in to see his editor that afternoon. Joey accompanied him, and the editor elevated disapproving eyebrows.

'This is Mr. King,' said Ace, 'the gentleman I asked you to put on the payroll as a junior reporter and my assistant on this assignment.'

'Hiya, boss!' said Mr. King respectfully.

'Merciful heavens!' moaned the editor. 'What next?' He raised his eyes to the ceiling as if seeking the answer from a higher source. No answer was vouchsafed him, and he turned to Ace again. 'I've got a lead for you on that night-club business,' he said. 'There's a place called The Silver Garter opened recently, and I believe the clientele is very select. You have to have a card to gain admission. I have a couple here that I borrowed from friends of mine. I understand there's some big-time gaming in the back room. Perhaps you will find the boss there.'

'Good!' said Ace, taking the cards. 'We had that place on schedule for tonight, but we didn't know about the cards.'

'By the way,' said the editor, eyeing the pair with ill-concealed disfavour, 'what are all these money items you keep drawing as 'incidental expenses'?'

'Let you know how I get on!' called back Ace, who seemed not to have heard the last remark. The door closed behind him. They ambled home to the flat and walked in.

Pudge Martin and the Dude rose from the armchairs they had been occupying and levelled their revolvers at the two.

'Afternoon, boys,' said. Ace with a smile. 'Should I work the old 'To what am I indebted for this visit'?'

The Dude grinned nastily. 'Sorry the acid gag didn't work out, Lannigan,' he remarked. 'But don't worry, old man! I've got a hundred just as good.'

'You boids sure have gotten a noive to bust in here like this,' gasped Mr. King.

'Don't tell me, my aristocratic friend,' mocked Ace, 'that you are going to attempt cold-blooded murder?'

The Dude flushed at the reference to his elegant ways. 'You know we aren't killers,' he remarked. 'But don't get the idea that we won't shoot in self-defence, old bean! The reason for our visit is simple.' He paused and his voice took on a steely rasp. 'Lay off, Lannigan,' he said, 'or else — '

'What?'

'The boss'll have you rubbed out!'

'Is that all?' asked Ace mildly.

The Dude nodded.

'Good! Then get this. If you and your blasted boss fancy you can rub me out, you're welcome to have as many goes as you like. You come here and threaten me? You, a weak-spined, gutless rat! You can tell the boss from me that I have no intention of laying off until I've cracked your racket wide open!' As he spoke, his hands, which had been resting on the edge of an occasional table, clenched; and to the surprise of the two mobsters, the table rose and was hurled violently against their chests. With startled exclamations they attempted to keep their balance, but Ace and Mr. King were on them and had wrenched the pistols from their gun hands.

There followed a brief struggle. Ace, who had tackled the Dude, quickly had his man down by twisting the injured hand which, although it did not prevent the Dude using a revolver, was still very sore. Mr. King had Pudge against the wall and was thudding the gangster's nose until Martin, too, was down.

Breathing heavily, Joey sat on his face. 'What now, boss?' he asked.

'Now,' Ace told him gravely, 'we bestow upon them the order of the boot!' He seized the reluctant Dude by the collar and jerked him to the open door.

Mr. King left Martin where he was and took up a position some two yards to the Dude's rear. At a word from Ace, he charged. A well-placed size eleven smote the gasping gangster on the seat of his too-elegant trousers, and with a shocked howl he commenced to shoot down the staircase, hitting the tenth, fifth, second and first steps respectively. Mr. Martin followed in like vein.

The two disgruntled racketeers dusted their clothes and proceeded painfully to the door, uttering improbable threats and dwelling in passing on the uncertainty of Mr. King's ancestry. They passed from view, wringing a surprised 'Goodness gracious me!' from the estimable Mrs. Hobson, who witnessed their going.

Slipping on a hat, Ace bade Joey a hasty adieu and followed them at a cautious distance. When he returned two hours later, he found Joey King spread-eagled on the settee with a large glass of whisky and a thoughtful expression.

'Joey,' he remarked, pouring himself a large glass also, 'I trailed those birds to none other than the Silver Garter. They thought they had thrown me off the scent by trotting into the Hotel Majestique and out at the other door again, dear boys. Tonight, Joey my lad, we are in for fun and games at the above-mentioned edifice.'

Mr. King stirred slothfully. 'Who's dat, boss?'

'Come again?'

'Who's dat guy? Do I know de nut?'

'Which nut?' demanded the puzzled Ace.

'Eddie Fizz!' said Joey plaintively.

Ace groaned soulfully. 'An edifice, my unlearned friend, is a structure, erection or building,' he volunteered.

'Geeze!' commented Joey. 'Ain't dere a heap to learn!'

6

Strip Poker at the Silver Garter

The Silver Garter night club opened for business as usual at nine that night. It was fairly crowded when the two Frenchmen arrived. They tendered their cards at the door and proceeded into a dining room-cum-dance hall, where several people were sitting at small glass-topped tables, drinking, and a few couples were revolving aimlessly in the confines of a roped-off square, which laboured to give the impression that it was a dance floor. A four-piece band (saxophone, drums, clarinet, and piano) was shrieking shrilly above the clatter of glasses and the hum of desultory conversation. An anemic-looking crooner was whispering 'Night and Day' into an oversized microphone.

The two Frenchmen were escorted to a table near the orchestra. About the leg of each table was a small silver garter, and the low bandstand was decorated so that the base resembled another garter. The two Frenchmen — one squat and solid with an immense beard and side whiskers (his conversation was confined to an abundance of '*oui*'s and '*n'est-ce pas*'s), and the other with a trim Van Dyke beard and 'tache (who conversed fluently in a mixture of French and broken English) — let it be understood by all in the vicinity that they were the new French ambassadors to England, 'on a mission the most important!' They also gave to all about the fact that they had already had '*un bour l'petit*', and they intended to 'a little more drink' before they took up their duties on the morrow.

Pudge Martin, attired in evening dress and trying to look like a gentleman, took careful note of all this. These, Pudge told himself, were a couple of suckers of the first water — just the type that he would love to get into his clutches — ambassadors! As the evening dragged on, he edged his way closer and closer to their table, seeking a convenient means of introduction. He found it — although it was hardly the means he would normally have chosen. He was standing at one corner of the foot-high dais from which the band were flinging their mournful banshee noises, when the younger Frenchman rose suddenly to his feet, lurched unsteadily rearwards and caught Pudge a nasty bump in the waistcoat with his elbow. The dais did the rest, for it caught Pudge on the calves, and he took a back-header into the big drum. The excited Frenchman fished him out, apologising profusely. The drummer gazed mournfully at his wrecked apparatus and tut-tutted with extreme annoyance. The youngish Frenchman escorted Mr. Martin to his table, doubling that worthy's arm and prodding his leg spasmodically to determine the nature of any injuries sustained.

'*Mon ami*,' he exclaimed feverishly. 'It is that I have the broken leg or arm caused to you. Yes!'

'Naw!' said Mr. Martin, his accent betraying his gentlemanly dress. 'Nope! I guess I'm still in the one lump!'

'Ah,' babbled the Frenchman. 'It is of an occurrence the most — unique, that

that one there — ' He now addressed his friend. ' — is insured not, Gaston.'

'*Oui, oui!*' agreed Gaston, twirling his beard.

'By my beard,' continued the first Frenchman, 'I am glad that his arm it works still.' Here he seized the arm in question and pumped it vigorously up and down, finally flinging it to his companion, who did likewise. Pudge waited for the performance to conclude, which was not for some seconds.

'Messoors are looking for some fun?' he then asked.

'Fun!' the Frenchman seized upon the magical word. '*Oui!* Is it that m'sieu could direct us to a place where we might have of fun the most excellent?'

'Women?' said Pudge with a sly glance at them.

'La, la!' The Frenchman raised his eyes to heaven in unholy ecstasy. His 'la, la' was fraught with deep meaning. 'That I like.'

'Churchay lar fern!' said Mr. Martin with an obnoxious wink.

'*Bien, bien!*' the Frenchman assured

him. 'My name, m'sieu — it is Pierre.'

'I'm Martin,' said Pudge. 'Pudge to you chaps.'

'Pooge? Pooge! It is well.' He seized Mr. Martin's suffering hand again and subjected it to a violent flinging. 'And now — *Vive 'la femme.''*

'Come with me,' said Mr. Martin mysteriously. He took them through a door behind the bandstand and through a room where gambling of all descriptions was in progress. Here the two Frenchmen would have stayed, but Pudge had better plans in store. The journey finished in a small well-furnished room at the rear of the club. Here Pudge bade them be seated, and he retired, to return after a minute with a bottle of fine champagne.

He brought with him four glasses, and as he poured out the liquid two women entered. They were pretty women of a cheap type, and they immediately draped themselves lovingly across the knees of the two foreigners. The Frenchmen appeared to be well pleased with them, and with a complete lack of ceremony commenced to justify the reputation of

Frenchmen as great lovers.

Pudge then produced a pack of cards. 'You play poker?' he asked.

'Pokairre?' said Pierre. 'We do not play, do we, Gaston?'

'*Oui, oui!*' said Gaston.

'What it is — this pokairre?' begged Pierre.

'Well, the way we play it,' said the woman on his knee, 'you take your clothes off when you lose!'

'It is good! You remove your *jupe?*' he said, pointing to her skirt. 'Good! You shall teach us!'

Pudge left the room, and with the light dimmed the game commenced. Within ten minutes the game had been contrived so that all four had removed their outer garments, the Frenchmen laughing uproariously. Then there was a sudden flash.

'What was that?' asked Pierre suspiciously.

The women shook their heads to indicate that they did not know. In the next room, Pudge Martin chuckled gleefully over the camera that had snapped the licentious scene.

'French ambassadors,' he muttered with a grin. 'I'll make them pay through the nose for these photos.'

Meanwhile in the other room, the party had split up. The Frenchmen seemed to have lost interest, and shortly afterwards they rolled out of the club, singing merrily.

'And if that doesn't produce a clue for us,' said Ace to Mr. King as they removed their beards and make-up in the privacy of his apartment, 'I'm a Dutchman.'

'Yeah, but how will they know how to find us?' said Joey.

'I made sure I let our dear Pudge hear we were staying at the Hotel Charles, and I have arranged for us to occupy a room there for a couple of days, We move in tomorrow. It should be very comfortable at the Hotel Charles,' he added.

As he had prophesied, it was comfortable. They took up their residence the following morning and spent a lazy day waiting for some sign from the gangsters.

It arrived on the second day in the shape of Mr. Pudge Martin, who bore in his pocket two snapshots. He also bore a note, typewritten and unsigned:

* * *

Gentlemen, I am sure that two such eminent men as yourselves would not care for the snapshots — which my assistant has — to be published in any paper or magazine, or publicly distributed among your contemporaries. In which case, it is advisable for you to hand my assistant the sum of £2,000 (English pounds), when you will receive the negative of the snaps you will be shown.

* * *

The note was unsigned and bore no address. Ace, disguised once more as Pierre, inspected the negatives and snaps. They were excellently clear and revealed the two men in a state of nature (almost) embracing two women, similarly clad.

'How about it?' said Pudge impudently. For answer, Ace went to his bedroom and let out the two police inspectors who had been listening to the conversation. The blackmailer was led off, fuming. The trail had been unsuccessful. Ace had hoped that the boss in person might have communicated with him, but it was not so. Apparently the boss was taking no chances.

That night the Silver Garter was raided by the police and closed down for good, but no trace of the owner was found. The boss had beat it for parts unknown.

★   ★   ★

In a small office off the Brixton Road, Dude Hays reclined in an immense chair behind a brand-new oak desk. On the frosted glass of the office door an inscription read: 'A. Fitzmaurice — Theatrical Agent — Continental Enterprises and Foreign Touring Agent.'

That morning the paper had contained one of Mr. Hays's advertisements: a carefully worded affair in which he stated that he was desirous of contacting beautiful show women, without existing ties in England, for protracted continental tours at the best playhouses. Once the women he snared reached the continent, they were heard of no more: it was an old game, a branch of the white slave traffic, and Dude was eternally surprised by the number of women who fell for his tales.

He interviewed three prospective victims that very morning. Secretly he was a little uneasy in his mind. He knew that if Ace Lannigan spotted his game, he would go the same way as Harry, Charlie, and lastly Pudge. Of course, he sported now his little black moustache and a brand new plain glass monocle, but Ace knew these things from brushes they had had in America: they were the set trademarks of the Dude's egoistical personality. The morning jacket and the sponge bag pants were familiar to every G-man in the States. These things were Dude Hays!

With an uneasy sigh, he dismissed his forebodings. Could he have seen Ace at that moment, he would have closed his office and given the white slaving a miss for a while.

★　★　★

Ace was having breakfast in bed again. He had before him a copy of the paper, and he was studying the Dude's enlightening little advertisement.

'Tut-tut!' he murmured to himself. 'If I hadn't seen it, I'm blowed if I'd have believed it! What a thoughtful chap the Dude is to let me know his little game!' He laid the paper down and gave himself up to thought. So far as he could see, Dude would never get him any nearer to discovering the identity of the boss, who plainly took no chances. To Ace, the delay in getting to grips with the unknown was irritating in the extreme. Slowly but surely he was polishing off the existing gang. Harry Benham, Charlie Gubbins, Pudge Martin — all these were back numbers now, and there remained only Dude Hays and the widow — and of course the boss.

He was blissfully unaware that the *Goliath* had again docked that very morning, and that on board had been three fresh imports — American hoodlums of the worst order, killers to the last man, to swell the numbers of the rapidly depleted gang. Also he was unaware of the three English crooks whom Mrs. Rafferty had enrolled in the service of the boss.

Ace dined at the Ritz. His meal was barely concluded when a middle-aged woman swept across the room and fell upon his neck, gushing thanks and praise. She was accompanied by a young woman. Ace recognised them as the Duchess of Deemstown and her delightful young secretary.

'Oh, my dear — *dear* — man!' babbled the duchess. 'I never did get the opportunity to thank you for rescuing me from those — those horrible, horrible gangsters. Such a brave, brave action!'

'Oh, my dear, dear duchess,' said Ace with a grin, 'it was nothing — nothing at all!' He exchanged a wink with the secretary.

'But it was!' panted the duchess. 'My friends were thrilled — thrilled, my dear man, when I told them.'

'Please forget it, my dear duchess,' reiterated Ace.

'I do *so* want to introduce you to my friends,' gushed the duchess. 'Tonight I'm throwing a big party, and just everybody will be there — it would be so nice if you would come, my dear Mr. Lannigan. Do say you will.'

She paused, gasping hoarsely for breath, and behind her back the secretary nodded. It was that smile and nod that decided Ace. Here was a woman in a million. He thought somewhat ruefully of Gloria Evans, then dismissed her with a slight shrug. Ace's offhanded dismissal of a woman he had been exceptionally fond of was typical of him, but he had actually done her a favour. She eventually found a nice office manager to marry, and was far happier with him than she would have been with the swashbuckling Ace.

'I think I will be able to make it, Duchess,' said Ace, and the duchess nearly had an apoplectic fit all over the floor of the Ritz. Still gushing furiously, the overjoyed woman took her secretary and her departure.

According to the duchess, the party was to be an informal affair at her town house in Berkeley Square, and thither at nine that night Ace repaired.

There was an orchestra playing old-fashioned waltzes, a running buffet, and a bar at which Ace lodged himself and did not budge. The duchess spotted him in no time, and he was quickly surrounded by a host of admiring elderly females who threatened to monopolise him to the exclusion of all others. After a while the duchess bustled about her business as hostess, and Ace sought sanctuary in the men's room. Here he remained for ten minutes, and as he protruded a cautious head he beheld the duchess's secretary standing by the open windows. With a rare turn of speed, Ace swept from his place of concealment, scooped her into his arms, and slid into the garden. There he released her, surprised and somewhat breathless, by a bench and sat down beside her.

'Mr. Lannigan! What on earth made you do that?'

'I wanted to see you about a little matter,' Ace said.

'What little matter was that?' she asked curiously.

'This!' said Ace, bending over and kissing her. For a second she seemed to pull away; then, discretion thrown to the wind, she returned the embrace.

'I'll bet you do that to all the women,' she said as Ace released her.

'No,' said Ace seriously. 'Only the good-looking ones.'

They laughed and began to talk in low tones, Ace thrilling her with blatantly immodest stories of his successes in America. The time flew, and when Ace glanced at his watch it was 11:30.

'She's a dear old soul,' Elsa said when Ace kidded her about the Duchess, 'and I'd rather be secretary to a fussy old Duchess than a middle-aged businessman with a fat paunch and an idea that because he pays your wages he owns you, lock, stock and all the rest of it.'

They could hear the Duchess of Deemstown approaching the terrace. Her remarks indicated that she was looking for Ace in order to introduce him to another bunch of friends. Ace stood up and announced his intention of going before she got on the scene.

'Ace,' said Elsa, 'you can't just walk out like that! What shall I tell the duchess?'

'Tell her,' he said, 'that I had an urgent

appointment with Hedy Lamarr.' He swung himself nimbly to the top of the wall. 'I'll see you for lunch at the Savoy at 2:30 tomorrow, honey!' And with a low laugh he had gone, leaving Elsa sitting there.

7

Ace, King, Queen

The scheme to trap the Dude, which Ace outlined to Mr. King and Elsa Daly the following day at lunch, was elementary.

'Why not just inform the police?' asked Elsa.

'Time enough for that after I have been through the Dude's safe and private papers,' Ace told her. 'I might possibly pick up some clues to the identity of the boss.'

The scheme was put into operation immediately. That same afternoon, Elsa Daly called on Mr. Fitzmaurice in his dingy office.

'Yes,' said Mr. Fitzmaurice, alias the Dude, gazing at her shapely limbs with licentious eyes, 'of course I can find continental work for you, my dear. You are just the type we are looking for. I can place you at a salary of twenty pounds a week for one year. That tempts you, eh?'

'Oh, yes, sir!' said Elsa demurely. 'When can I expect to leave?'

'Oh, I'll let you know that later,' the Dude told her. 'Perhaps at the weekend, eh?'

Elsa hesitated and gazed at him with troubled eyes.

'What is it, my dear?'

'Only — only — I've been borrowing money from a friend,' she explained, 'and I don't like leaving without paying her.'

'How much have you gone into debt?'

'Fifty pounds!'

'Goodness me! That's a deuced lot of money for a young woman to owe. Never mind! Perhaps I can arrange an advance of fifty on your salary. I know what! Come and have a little supper with me tonight?'

Elsa hemmed and hawed. She wasn't sure — it didn't sound right; it didn't *seem* right. The Dude, fairly dripping with soft soap, talked her round. Of course it was right! Surely she didn't think . . . No, she told him, of course she didn't think *that*. It was just what *people* would think.

'Have you anyone very near to you?'

asked the Dude in surprise. 'You told me that your father and mother were dead and that you had no other relations.'

'That's right,' she said. 'Really, there isn't anyone who matters.'

'Well then,' said the Dude, 'that's all right! You come along to Nine Hampton Terrace tonight and I'll have fifty pounds for you, eh?' Finally she allowed herself to be persuaded and left, thanking the Dude profusely. She met Ace at the comer of the street.

'Nine o'clock,' she said. 'Nine Hampton Terrace. A little supper, fifty pounds, and who knows what else?'

'Fifty pounds!' whistled Ace. 'Hmm! The Dude must have a well-paying market for the women he picks up if he can afford to advance them fifty.'

'Of course, I suppose that includes the fee for his own little spot of entertainment!' she said.

'Yes,' said Ace. 'What a shock the dear lad will get! Ah, me! What a disappointment. And now,' he continued as they crossed to the Underground, 'we eat, drink and be merry, for tonight we deprive the Dude of his money and his liberty.'

* * *

Dude Hays was in his seventh heaven of anticipation. For the last half hour he had been bustling about, setting the scene for what he hoped would be a tender love scene culminating in the utter surrender of the young lady who owed her friend fifty pounds. Fifty pounds well spent, he considered, for her subsequent purchase by a Montmartre house of ill fame that would reimburse him to the extent of at least two hundred. Of this he was sure.

Once the woman was across the channel and had reported to the address he would give her, she would vanish from human ken, and there would be nothing in writing — nothing to point to the elite Dude as her abductor. Once in the hands of Madame Fiellou, she would be subjected to a treatment of drugs that would quickly relieve her of her memories and make her submissive to any treatment. The Dude had it all arranged: the small table with the flowers, the champagne, the soft romantic music issuing from the automatic radiogram, the simple supper set for two, the fifty pounds parked temptingly on the mantelpiece, and lastly the little packet of dope he would slip into her champagne. He rubbed his hands in high glee, and the bell clamoured shrilly.

'Come in, Miss Daly!' he said, opening the door with what he considered a fatherly smile.

She entered uncertainly, and the Dude relieved her of her coat. 'Please sit down. Shall we have supper at once?'

'It's a little early, isn't it, Mr. Fitzmaurice?'

'Oh, I don't know. Let's get the supper over with so that we can sit and talk.' He noticed the way her eyes crept to the money. 'Yes, I managed to get that for you.' He smiled.

They sat down to supper and speedily disposed of it, the Dude talking all the while in a manner calculated to set his intended victim at ease. He apparently succeeded, for she made no objections when he slipped an arm about her slender waist.

'Now the champagne, eh?' he said jovially. He carefully poured two glasses, and with his back to her slid the powder in one. 'Here you are, my dear! Finest money can buy!'

She drank it in little sips, and the gloating Dude watched her finish it to the last drop. He talked constantly and. encouragingly of the great success she would be in France, and slowly her head drooped and rested on his ready shoulder. She lost consciousness. Trembling, the Dude picked her up and carried her into the bedroom. Then he hastily returned through the lounge into the hall of his little flat and, taking his key, locked the door with excited fumbling fingers. Back through the lounge into the bedroom he went — and received a profound shock.

Ace Lannigan was sitting by the side of Elsa on the bed. 'Evening, Mr. Fitzmaurice,' he said politely.

'Lannigan!' stuttered the crook, his eyes popping from his sleek skull. 'How did you get here?'

'I nipped in when you first carried your little friend here into the bedroom, old bean. I was behind the curtains when you went through to lock the door, and here I am — what? You know, I'm surprised at you, Dude! Up to these little games at your age — you must be over forty!'

'I don't quite know what you mean, Lannigan. This lady is a personal friend of mine — '

'My dear chap! Are you in the habit of slipping your friends concentrated Mickeys?'

'I tell you she's a friend!' rapped the Dude savagely.

'Maybe — but does she know it? No, my friend; this young lady is here by a social arrangement — not by your special arrangement, Dude, but by mine!'

Dude Hays clenched his fists. He saw how easily he had had the wool pulled over his eyes.

'I'm afraid I was a little late in getting here,' said Ace, 'and I apologise. I had no idea you would slip her a snoozing draught so early. Really, you must have been impatient, Dude.' He fixed that unfortunate with a glittering eye.

'You're sticking your nose out too far, Lannigan. How much will you take to lay off?' He tried it as a last resort, and knew it was hopeless even as he suggested it, for a mocking laugh wrinkled the corners of Ace's mouth.

'I've taken it!' he said. 'Fifty quid from the mantelpiece. That's not hush money, brother! That's to repay me for all sorts of trouble you have caused me. It seemed to be lying about serving no purpose, so I collected it. Was that all right?'

'What are you going to do, Lannigan?' said Dude Hays harshly.

Ace grinned and crossed his legs carefully. 'You've had your run, Dude. Tell me who the boss is. No? Then I think we will just call that stout constable who patrols without.'

He saw the desperate resolve in the Dude's eyes as he spoke. He knew that the Dude was going to make a break for it; that the crook of the elegant monocle and toothbrush was not going to let the prison gates shut behind him if he could help it. He knew, too, from the way the Dude's clothes hugged his body that he had no weapons concealed about him. And, knowing all this, Ace felt a great gladness, and an urge for the chase to begin.

It began sooner than he had expected, for with a swift movement Hays switched off the light. Ace came to his feet with a bound and leapt after the Dude. He heard the bedroom door close, tore it open, and saw the open window immediately. In a second Ace was out in the night on the fire escape. He had been a little unwary, for instead of going down Hays had gone up; and as Ace peered after him, a lashing foot caught him on the temple. Ace drew his head in against the wall and tried to grab that foot, but Hays was on his way.

Blood poured into Ace Lannigan's eyes from an ugly cut on the forehead; he blinked and swept a hand across his brow, then he was ascending after his enemy. The fire escape terminated in a loose iron ladder which for the last three feet was flat to the side of the building. It was suspended by hooks from the wall. Ace had his hands halfway up this when the hooks were wrenched free, and for one awful moment Ace could visualise the nice burial his paper would give him, and the thought was not pleasing. He jumped. His clutching, clawed fingers hooked on the flat parapet and he pulled himself up. He obtained a hold on the unwary crook's trouser legs and pulled. Hays battered furiously at his face and shoulders and strove to tear loose that grip on the ends of his trousers, but Ace drew himself up steadily. Dazed, half-conscious from the rain of blows, Ace clung grimly and was dragged away from the edge of the roof.

The Dude was completely insane: his eyes glittered in the light of the full moon and he mouthed horrible words; his monocle dangled at the end of its cord, and he alternately shrieked and gibbered. A metal bar left by some workmen fell beneath his hand, and seizing it, he dashed it madly at the now-unconscious figure before him. It struck Ace on the back of the head, and his convulsive clutch on the madman's trousers loosened. The Dude, growling like a savage beast, picked him up and walked to the edge of the roof. Foam and blood fell on the figure he held from his open, slavering jaws. Ace was raised shoulder high —

Joey King, who had been waiting outside the Dude's flat in case he was needed, heard the turmoil on the roof. He spent some time looking for a way up, found it after wasting precious minutes, and arrived in time to see the mad crook carry his senseless victim to the edge of the roof. Crossing swiftly and silently, Joey wound a strong arm about Dude's throat and pulled him pell-mell backwards. Ace dropped to the floor, and the Dude struggled against that tightening grip. His foot jammed backwards into Joey's groin, and with a groan of agony Joey released him. The Dude was pulling at the same time, and his sudden release caught him off balance. He pitched towards the edge of the roof, and Joey saw his white face and terror in it. Then he was gone, his screams echoing piercingly back to the roof. Joey, listening intently, heard the thud . . .

The screams had ended. The Dude was no more. His splattered body lay at the foot of the building, his head cracked cleanly down the centre. Joey doubled up for a while to ease his agonised groin. The kick had almost crippled him.

'Geeze!' he said to himself. 'I guess I'd rather have a coupla rounds wid Joe Louis dan play round wid dat boid again.' Still suffering, he dragged Ace back into the building and burst open the door of the Dude's room.

He dialed Ace's newspaper first of all. Since joining up with Ace, Mr. King had learned that the story always came first!

★　★　★

The period of terror started the second day after Ace had been taken to the hospital suffering from head injuries. The London constabulary were hopelessly inadequate to deal with the armed gunmen who invaded their fair city, and the police cars could not match the speed of the superb American cars that had

255

been imported for the mobsters.

The first attack took place on a bank in Hammersmith. At about 11:30 in the morning, a car drove up and four men entered the bank. Two police constables on duty nearby noted the fact that one man sat at the wheel of the car and the engine remained running. This roused their suspicions, and they were prepared for what followed. A shot sounded within the bank, and the four gunmen backed out loaded with notes that had been hastily scooped into bags. One clerk who had resisted them lay dead. The two constables rushed them immediately, their truncheons ready for action. They were shot down out of hand; and, piling into the car, the gunmen escaped.

That was merely the start.

At 2:30 that afternoon, a well-known money-lender was shot dead in his office, and the contents of his safe were removed by a man who had apparently come to borrow money. His young secretary was brutally handled when she tried to telephone the police.

That same night, the Ballan Street

Branch Bank was broken into and burgled, the watchman being shot. The bank was then set on fire.

The second day a beautiful woman, daughter of a city financier, was kidnapped, and in due course a ransom demand for £50,000 made its appearance. The ransom was paid immediately by the anxious father, and the woman was found in a distressed condition five hours later, with no clear idea of what had occurred.

Stubborn officials reluctantly sent a chief inspector to interview Ace Lannigan, who was sitting up and taking notice.

'Mr. Lannigan,' said Chief Inspector Ronald Briggs, 'you know the ways of these thugs! Based on your own experiences in America, have you any suggestions on how to combat them?'

'First of all, you're dealing with killers,' said Ace, 'so the first step is to issue arms to your police force. Secondly, you have no body of men especially fitted to deal with these yobs. That means that you must form one. Model them on the lines of our federal agents and G-men. Thirdly,

I'll be out of here shortly and I may be of some help to you!'

With that, the inspector had to be satisfied; and so impressed were official ears by Lannigan's record that they immediately issued small arms to their London constables. The value of this action became apparent the following day. During the hold-up of a clerk who was carrying the wages for the staff of a large store, from the bank to that store, one of the hold-up men was shot dead by an armed constable, and yet another was badly wounded making his getaway.

The London scene quietened, and the gang transferred its attentions to the cotton city — Manchester. Here there occurred a repetition of the raids that had shocked London. Hold-up, kidnap, murder! The scene of operations moved ever faster — there was no way of telling where a fresh outrage would occur. Sheffield felt the cold cruelty of the mobsters; then Bradford, Leeds and Liverpool. The total of deaths rose by leaps and bounds. It was crime gone mad. Then, as suddenly as it had begun, the Time of Terror ended.

Ace Lannigan left hospital a few days later, his head still swathed with bandages. The editor, Michael Woodson, was waiting for him on the step and the two shook hands, for the editor had been too busy to pay him a visit for the three previous days.

There was also a plain ambulance at the kerb, and a young man in a white medical smock crossed over to them. 'Mr. Lannigan?' he asked.

'Sure, that's me.'

'The police have sent instructions that you are to be taken home in this ambulance, to eliminate any chance of the mobsters trying to get you. If you'll just hop in the back, no one will be able to tell that it is the famous Ace Lannigan leaving hospital.'

'Here, wait a second!' said Michael Woodson. 'I've got the press car parked out here.'

'It's no use taking chances,' said Ace. 'I'll go in the ambulance. You follow on in the press car.' It was arranged thus; and, Ace being safely installed in the back of the ambulance, it drove rapidly away.

Woodson climbed leisurely into the press car and pressed the starter. He was about to pull out when a police car whizzed round the corner, braked, and Chief Inspector Briggs came out. 'Hello, Woodson,' he said. 'Where's Lannigan?'

The editor looked surprised. He knew Briggs slightly from his reporting days. 'He just left in the ambulance you sent for him!'

Briggs, tensed. 'Who sent for him?' he snapped. 'We just came to pick him up and see him safely home!'

'You didn't send a plain ambulance for him?' asked the amazed editor.

'You mean to say he fell for that old gag?' demanded the thoroughly startled inspector. 'Which way did he go, man? Quick!'

Woodson pointed and Briggs dived back into the police car. It roared away. Worried, Michael Woodson drove to the reporter's flat. There was no sign of Ace Lannigan. Inside the flat Mr. King had been sitting on the settee, waiting. When Woodson arrived he jumped up and admitted him.

'Where's de boss?' he demanded, puzzled.

'He's been abducted again!' said Woodson wearily. 'He's been kidnapped right under my eyes. Where's the phone? I want to get the story in for the next edition!' Joey collapsed weakly on the settee. 'Geeze!' he murmured.

8

'Not Cricket!'

When Ace had stepped into that ambulance, he had had a vague premonition; an uneasy feeling that something was haywire. The young white-coated medico had closed the doors behind him and Ace had been left in darkness, for the ambulance possessed no windows or ventilation that he could see. He tried the doors and found that they opened only from the outside. The motor started up, and Ace could hear the sound of the wheels whirring over the tarmac. His head was aching infernally. He knew definitely that he was being snatched from under the very eyes of the police and his editor, for the ambulance had been travelling too long now to have been still in London. All the noises of the heavily crowded London traffic could no longer be heard.

He tried to batter the doors down with his feet, but the rear compartment of the pseudo-ambulance was constructed of plate steel. Then he became aware of something else. It was a peculiar smell, and he knew it to be gas. He fumbled about the walls for the inlet pipe and failed to discover it. He gave up and sat on a bunk arrangement with his back to the wall. The fumes grew intense. Ace Lannigan lost consciousness . . .

The ambulance roared on and on at top speed. The alarm had gone out by now, and though the driver avoided any towns, he was compelled to crash through a road block, badly injuring the two men who stood before it waving their arms.

They were in the heart of the country now, and the man who sat by the driver switched off the gas that had been pouring into the back of the ambulance. 'Listen, Al,' he said, 'what's the idea of kidnapping this man Lannigan?'

'How the hell should I know?' retorted his companion. 'We got the job to do and he's got to be rubbed out, see? I don't know who's going to do the bumpin'. We just gotta take the mug down to the house.' His intonation was American, and he was well known in the midwestern states as Two Gun Al. His companion was an Englishman known to the police as Slick Benny. The ambulance bumped on, and in the back Ace remained unconscious. Eventually somewhere in Essex it drew up, and the two men climbed out, the Englishman shedding his medical smock. They opened the rear doors and yanked out the senseless Ace.

'Where'll we dump him?' asked Benny.

'I guess the cellar would be best. He's a slippery cuss!' Ace was duly deposited in the windowless cellar. The kidnappers returned to a front room overlooking the grass-grown lawn. Here there were a couple of billiard tables, and four men were desultorily knocking the balls about.

'You get him?' asked one, looking up.

'Yep!' Al assured him. 'Easy as smelling a skunk!'

'What now?' inquired another of the gang.

Al shrugged. 'That's up to the dame,' he said. 'She said she'd be here around four an' it's on that now.' As he spoke the door opened, and Mrs. Rafferty walked in.

'Where is he?' she asked with no word of greeting.

'He's in the cellar,' said Al. 'You want me to bump him off?'

'No, the boss wants that privilege.' The mobsters blinked. This was the first intimation they had had since they had been contacted in America that they were working for someone other than Rafferty's wife. The English crooks were also surprised.

'Bring him up here,' said Rafferty. 'I'd like to talk to him. Tie him up well first. He has a peculiar knack for getting out of the tightest corners.'

Al and Benny left the room.

'Mr. Lacey — and you, Mr. Faming — had better go with them in case he has recovered consciousness.' The two men indicated nodded and followed Al and Benny. Then Rafferty turned to the remaining two. 'How are you gentlemen getting on?' she asked.

The two Englishmen frowned. 'Not so

badly, thanks,' said one.

'Except for these killings that your American friends are pulling off,' said the other. 'Personally, I don't like it! Sooner or later the police will catch up with us, and then . . . ' He left the sentence unfinished.

Rafferty nodded. 'That's a chance you must take. But don't think too hard of Al and his friends. After all, their business is murder, just as murder is the business of a professional soldier. They are there to protect you, gentlemen, while you carry out my orders.'

'I don't quite get the comparison between the boys and a professional soldier,' said the taller of the men. 'At least a soldier doesn't shoot down unarmed men! That's what I don't like!'

Rafferty's face hardened. 'You are not here to like or dislike!' she said harshly. 'You will either do as I tell you, or . . . ' she nodded in the direction Al had gone.

The Englishmen wisely held their silence.

The four men returned with Ace Lannigan. There had obviously been a tussle, for Al's eye was turning a gorgeous purple and Benny sported a split lip. The bandage about Ace's head had assumed a disreputable shade and was hanging loosely. Ace, his own cheek blossoming out into a deep purple, smiled a cheery smile. 'Well!' he remarked. 'As I live and breathe — so far, the charming Widder Rafferty in person.'

'Good evening, Mr. Lannigan. I trust we have not inconvenienced you in any way?'

'No, no,' said Ace carelessly. 'As a matter of fact, I adored that little combined room in the cellar. It didn't smell as much as it does up here.'

Rafferty flushed.

'Aha!' mocked Ace. 'Maiden modesty has you in its grip, Mrs. R.!'

'Please try to stand the objectionable odour you refer to, Mr. Lannigan,' she rejoined. 'I assure you it was not detectable before you yourself graced us with your presence. Besides, we have arranged what we hoped might be a little pleasant entertainment for you, to occupy that enquiring mind of yours until the boss arrives.'

'Ah me, yes — the elusive boss. Quite a work of fiction, this boss of yours, Mrs. Rafferty. I do get tired of waiting, though.'

'Good things come to those who wait,' said Rafferty seriously, 'and I don't think you will have long to wait now, my friend.'

She had crossed to his chair as she spoke. During this duologue, the Americans had bound him firmly to his chair again. It was a heavy Chesterfield. Rafferty suddenly ripped off his bandages and Ace winced.

'Obviously we are about to indulge in laughter and frolics — what!' he said lightly.

She smiled grimly, the mockery gone from her eyes. 'Frolics? Perhaps! But no laughter, Ace Lannigan. Not for you. I wish to teach you that it is unwise to interfere with honest crooks trying to make a living. I wish to know a thing or two. You will tell me, my friend. First, who was your accomplice in the capture of Dude Hays?'

'Oh, yes,' said Ace thoughtfully. 'You

remember Joey King? Well, believe it or not, it was Joey disguised!'

'Please don't lie. Mr. Hays would have hardly considered King a likely subject for — '

'Seduction and abduction?' asked Ace. 'You know, I think the monocle the poor dear Dude wore impaired his vision.'

'Mr. Lannigan, I hardly think that you are being truthful. Come, now. Or shall I turn you over to the boys?'

'Yeah!' rumbled Al. 'We're wastin' time. Let's give the sap the works!'

'You may — unless Mr. Lannigan has changed his mind?'

'No,' said Ace. 'By all means, turn me over to your freshly imported murderers.'

'As you will,' said Rafferty. 'You once endeavoured to extract information from the late Mr. Benham. You played on his injured leg, I imagine. Therefore you can have no objection to our making use of the wound on your head? No, of course not. I think I will leave the room and wait elsewhere. Al, you know what you have to find out. You may entertain our mutual friend.' She left the room gracefully, and

Al took off his jacket and rolled up his sleeves.

Ace tensed himself. *Wham!* Al's flat hand cracked on the scarcely healed wound on Ace's head. He jerked forward against his bonds. *Slap!* This time the blow took him on the forehead and Ace winced. Al clenched his fist. His bunched knuckles took Ace between the eyes. Ace gave a coughing grunt and tightened his lips.

'How about it,' asked Al, 'before I really get going? Who was the dame who helped you put the Dude under?'

'Didn't you read the papers?' said Ace thinly.

'Papers didn't give no names but yours.'

'That's good! It looks like you've got no way of finding out.'

Al took him by the throat and slowly began to throttle. He let go and pulled Ace's hair until his throat was stretched taut, then hit Ace's throat with his clenched fist. He seized his arms and twisted them savagely, then his fist thudded in the tortured man's stomach.

Ace was violently sick. They untied him from the chair and stood him on his feet. Al's fist travelled forward and smashed into Ace's face; and the reporter hurled across the room. Next Al took a heated poker from the fire. The two Americans held Ace against the wall and Al drew the poker across his head wound briskly. 'Talk!' he snarled. The poker approached again . . .

'Hang on, damn it!' snapped one of the Englishmen. 'You're going a bit too far!'

The three Americans whirled and stared at the speaker. Ace, released, slumped to the floor.

'What's eatin' you, Pantywaist?' said Al dangerously.

The Englishmen drew together. 'I said you were going too far,' said the man addressed as Pantywaist. 'An' I repeat it! Your third-degree methods aren't very pretty. We have different ways of doing things. You thugs have no sense of fair play.'

'Who the hell are you to talk about fair play?' bawled Al. 'You cheap crook!'

'Crook I may be,' said the Englishman

steadily. 'But, thank God, we haven't got any crooks like you in England. At least not English-born. This trouble isn't just over Lannigan! It's been in the wind a good time now. We don't like your methods, and we won't stand by and see you torture an injured man any longer.'

'Do you think Lannigan wouldn't do the same to you? How about what he did to that guy Benham you heard about?'

'From what I hear, Benham deserved all he got. Anyway, it isn't a question of what Lannigan would do! He's an American, too. I tell you there'll be trouble here if you can't leave him alone!'

Al looked nonplussed. The Englishmen were grimly sincere. Their faces were taut and ready for trouble: they had been forced to be parties to crimes which made even them shudder, but they had reached the limit. Cold-blooded murder they might stand for. Torturing an injured man was something different again.

'We're through!' said the Englishman; a revolver had sprung into his hand. 'We'll take the money and leave you boys to it!'

Blank looks had appeared on the

Americans. 'Is this a double cross?' demanded Al incredulously.

'That's about it,' agreed the man with the gun. Benny had scurried to the table, and from beneath it he took a large bag that contained the ill-gotten gains of the gang.

'You won't pull it off,' said Al. 'We'll get you, Landon. I thought this was going to happen.'

'That's all right,' said Landon. 'We can take our chances. If we stick with you, we're sure to wind up on the gallows. While we're at it, we'll take Lannigan. I shouldn't care to leave him with you gentlemen after this. You might take it out on him.' The other Englishman picked up the relieved Lannigan and draped him across one shoulder.

'Now we will take our leave before the lady returns,' said Landon. And take their leave they did, locking the door on the Americans. They commandeered the ambulance that had brought Ace. The Americans were trying to break down the heavily shuttered windows of the room they were locked in, but the ambulance was well out of the vicinity before they succeeded.

The four of them, including Ace, were jammed into the front seats of the ambulance. They had progressed about ten miles when Ace proved that he had a large amount of gratitude.

'Just a second!' he gasped as one of the Englishmen was clumsily re-bandaging his burn. 'You guys are running smack into trouble!'

'How's that?' asked Landon, giving him a curious glance.

'This ambulance,' said Ace. 'Boy, it'll be smoking hot! Every flatfoot in Britain'll be looking out for it, and when they find it you boys are going to get hooked — if you're still in it.'

'That's right, Gerry!' said Benny excitedly. 'Gee, what dopes we were to take this truck.'

Landon nodded. 'Thanks for the tip! I think we'll dump the ambulance here. We have no grudge against you, Lannigan. In fact, the way you took that beating I rather admire you. We'll leave you here, and if you like you can take the ambulance.'

'Aren't you a bit worried in case I report your descriptions to the Yard?' asked Ace.

'Not at all! We have an excellent hide-out and really I don't think you will, will you?'

'I reckon I won't at that,' agreed Ace.

The three men climbed out of the ambulance. Ace started the ambulance again.

'If you *do* report to the Yard,' shouted Landon, 'remember me to Inspector Briggs. Tell him Slippery Landon was asking after his health and hoping it was not too good!'

Ace managed a grin. 'I hope I'll meet up with you guys again someday,' he shouted, 'when we're not on business.'

'Hey,' yelled Landon suddenly, 'wait a minute!'

Ace grinned as he stepped on the petrol. 'Sorry about the bag, boys,' he chuckled to himself, 'but it'll be safer with me.' He glanced complacently at the bag full of notes that the men had forgotten in their hurry, and, still grinning, he vanished from their outraged eyes.

* * *

'You're telling me,' said Chief Inspector Ronald Briggs in exasperation, 'that you were kidnapped, put to sleep, beaten up, branded with a red-hot poker, and ditched by the roadside in an ambulance with £500,000 in a bag, *without* regaining consciousness?'

Ace lazily lit a cigarette. 'That's it, Inspector. Silly, isn't it?'

'*Too* damned silly,' agreed Briggs. 'We're grateful for the return of the money, but at least tell us what happened to you. It may help us. If you don't, Lannigan, I'm formally warning you that you run the risk of becoming an accessory after the fact!'

'Quit kidding, Inspector,' said Ace sleepily. 'What I told you goes, and I'd take it kindly if you'd collect that bag and go yourself. Not that I want to be so infernally rude, but my head aches likes the very devil!'

Chief Inspector Ronald Briggs rose with a sigh. 'Very well, Lannigan. I'll call again.'

'Please do, Inspector. By the way, I met a charming chap called Slippery Landon. He asked to be remembered to you and hoped your health was failing.'

Briggs spun round. 'What!' he roared. 'Where the hell — where'd you see Landon?'

'Just bumped into him along the road,' said Ace. 'Goodbye, Inspector!'

★   ★   ★

'Look here, boss,' said Mr. King later, 'why for geeze sakes didn't youse tell that busy who snatched youse?'

'No, thanks!' Ace replied. 'I've got a personal score to settle with Al and his little chums. They won't see the inside of a cell until I've played their own game with them. Besides, they aren't so stupid that they would stay in that house any longer.' He paused and smiled. 'There's one thing, though. These birds must be a boon and a blessing to house agents — if they're paying for the dumps they use.'

9

A Nice Quiet Evening

Ace called for Elsa the following day at the duchess's town house. The duchess was unaware of the part Elsa had played in the annihilation of the Dude. Neither Ace nor Elsa had thought it fit to tell her.

Before they could make their escape, the Duchess had spotted and swooped over Ace and was telling him how terribly thrilled she had been by his latest exploits. This process occupied at least half an hour, and might have continued indefinitely had not the duchess had another appointment.

However, to their relief, it finally came to an end; and having escaped, they directed their footsteps towards the London Regal. Here the queues stretched for innumerable miles. Disheartened, they turned to fresh fields, eventually coming to roost in the Flickadrome. The film showing was a gangster story and Ace reveled in it. They were seated in the circle and a short interval was observed between the two features, during which Ace excused himself and slipped outside to the toilet, in order to take some aspirin for his still-delicate head. It was at this time that he sensed he was being followed by a well-dressed elderly man. He returned to the circle puzzled, and had hardly taken his seat again when his shadow crept in and resumed the seat immediately behind. It was the clumsiest shadowing Ace had ever seen. He purposely left during the performance of the second feature, and on the way to the duchess's house he again noted the presence of that shadow.

He had no fear of being shot at, for it was plain from the number of times that he had been in the mobsters' clutches that this job was to be left entirely to the boss — whoever that might be. He left Elsa at the corner of the road, bestowing a hasty good-night kiss upon her.

He deliberately elected to walk home, having no desire to lose his shadow. He went straight up to his flat and switched on the light. Then he rapidly descended the rear staircase, ran round the back of the block, and came out at the end of the street. As he suspected, the shadow was halfway along the street, watching intently. For about ten minutes the man watched; then, as there were no signs of Ace leaving the building again, he turned and made his way from the street. Ace, coat collar upturned, followed cautiously. He was a superb master of the shadowing art. How many times he had gumshoed down a New York slum area in search of copy would be hard to say; his experience stood him in good stead.

The shadower was unaware that the tables were turned: that he was now the shadowed; to the best of his knowledge Ace was in his flat, preparing to retire. Therefore he received a great shock when, turning down a slummy entry in Limehouse, a vice-like hand caught him by the throat.

'Pause awhile, friend!' breathed Ace softly.

The man let out a yip of terror. In the gloom he was unable to see his assailant.

'What — what do you want?' he gasped. 'I haven't any money.'

Ace grinned. 'What was the idea of following me?'

The captive jumped. 'I don't understand.'

'Oh yes, you do! I want to get the lowdown on this tailing you've been doing, pal.'

'Who — who are you?'

'You know who I am,' said Ace. 'Now talk — while you're still able to!'

'You leave me alone,' said the man indignantly. 'I'll have the law on you!'

'I doubt it, but it may be worth a try to you. If I'm not mistaken, there'll be a bobby at the end of this street.' He waited, but no call was forthcoming. 'I thought not,' said Ace, and he presented the shivering prisoner with a bunch of knuckles in the teeth. The man moaned and spat blood. He was moved to retaliation. It was unfortunate for Ace that he failed to spot the razor till it had gashed open his hand. He spotted it then quickly enough, and without releasing the man's neck slammed his head against the wall.

Ace jammed a foot on the open razor, which had dropped from his victim's fingers. He became aware of the bobby he had mentioned advancing upon them.

'What's goin' on 'ere?' asked that worthy, drawing quite close to Ace and the now unconscious shadower.

'It's quite all right, officer,' said Ace, keeping his foot firmly on the razor. 'My friend here has had a little too much to drink.'

'Well, 'e can't stop 'ere. I'll give you an 'and to get 'im to a taxi, sir.'

Ace cursed beneath his breath. The constable took hold of the supposed drunk, then suddenly gave a startled exclamation. ''Ell fire! 'Is 'ead's bleedin'!'

'I know. He bumped it coming out of the club.'

The constable shook his head and bent to look closer. 'I'm afraid I'll 'ave to take you along to the station — ' he said, and stopped because Ace's fist had rendered it impossible for to continue by smiting him violently on the nape of the neck. Ace judged that he would be senseless for some little time.

'I think your London policemen are too inquisitive,' Ace said to nobody in particular. He shook the man in his grip and was answered by a feeble groan. 'I don't like guys who play with razors,' he said, 'and I'm here to give you more of the last dose if you can't talk!' He wondered if the man was the boss for the minute, but dismissed the idea as very improbable. It was not like the boss to take a chance.

The frightened man was finally talking. The gist of it was that he had been engaged to trail Lannigan and keep his employer informed of any suspicious moves that the reporter made. His employer was a woman. He was to meet her each night and report in a little club at the end of this alley.

'All right,' Ace said. 'But if I catch you hanging around again, I'll probably kill you!' He released his hold and the man made haste to vanish into the shadows further along the street. Ace knew he would be too busy attending to his injuries to bestow any more attention on less important matters. The reporter turned up his coat collar and hauled his trilby over his eyes. He tied a handkerchief tightly about his sliced hand.

The entrance to the club consisted of a blank wooden door at the end of the entry. Leaving the still-dreaming policeman where he was, Ace made his way towards it. He knocked. The door was opened cautiously about two inches on a chain.

'What yer want?' asked a Cockney voice.

'I got a message for a bitter fluff,' said Ace, passably imitating the Cockney accent.

'Wot's the parsword?'

'I don't know no parsword. A bloke wot jest got hailed in by the narks, 'e told me as 'ow if I brought this message wot 'e give me to a woman in this 'ere club she'd see me orlright.'

'Garn,' said the doorman. ''Oo the 'ell yer kidden? Wot's the woman's nime?'

'Missus Rafferty!' said Ace.

The doorman eyed him closely. 'Come in!' he said, and opened the door. Ace felt the quick surge of blood and excitement in his veins. He was going into action again.

He entered and the door was locked behind him. The man indicated a little passage and a door at the end of it. 'Along there,' he said.

Trying to seem nonchalant, Ace negotiated it. The door opened to his touch and he stepped in.

'Good evening,' said Mrs. Rafferty. She was sitting facing the door he had entered through, and behind her clutching their guns were the three American thugs.

'You stick that neck of yours out too far, Lannigan,' she went on. 'We knew that if you fancied you were being shadowed, you'd almost certainly trail the shadower. That's why we allowed that blundering idiot you saw to do the shadowing. In actual practice I doubt if he could shadow an elephant without it knowing. I see by your hand that he got a little rough with you.'

'I got a little rougher with him,' Ace told them.

'Of course, I didn't really know that you would handle him before he had reached his destination. Suppose he had refused to talk?'

'Since there's only one door in the entry, it was plain where his destination would be.'

'I'm afraid that you will have no chance to escape this time!' she told him gravely. 'All right, Sam!'

Her eyes were looking over Ace's shoulders, and too late he remembered the man who had admitted him. Then his sadly damaged head received another blow . . .

*   *   *

Mr. Joey King had been hard at work that night. When Ace had dashed up to his apartment and switched on the lights, Mr. King had been lying half asleep on the settee. Ace's sudden arrival and re-departure had caused him to sit up and take notice. He had followed Ace out of the rear entrance and had been just in time to witness his boss commence to shadow a man. In his turn, and not wishing to attract attention to Ace by making himself known, he had shadowed the man who was shadowing the shadower. He had seen the little tussle from across the road and he had seen Ace strike the policeman. Then Ace had vanished; and Joey, on crossing over, had found only the policeman, who was lying as if poleaxed.

The door at the end of the entry had opened, and Mr. King drew into the deep shadows. A man Joey had not seen before came out and ran hurriedly down the road. He was not gone long and he returned driving a heavily curtained car. The door opened again, and once more Mr. King hugged the shadows while his startled eyes witnessed Ace, now unconscious, being carried to the car. With him was a woman and two more men. The three climbed into the closed car and shut the doors behind them. The engine burst into life and the car rolled away — with Mr. King hanging tooth and nail on the spare tyre at the rear.

10

The Boss at Last

Ace tried to ease his aching arms by standing on tiptoe. How long exactly he had hung like this he had no idea. He had been hanging when he regained consciousness and he had hung ever since.

He was in a small barn. Hay was plentifully distributed about the floor, and sheaves of it were stocked in the low loft. A number of farming tools were strewn in the corners of the barn, and on an upturned plough sat the three gangsters. Rafferty had remained leaning against the side of the barn, and Ace just hung. His wrists were firmly tied, as were his ankles. His arms were pulled upright till they were almost leaving their sockets, for the rope that held them was fastened to a hook in the wall. It was a favourite Eastern method of torture, and it eliminated any chance of escape. His repeated efforts to draw Mrs.

Rafferty out had failed. Illumination was provided by an oil lamp suspended from the edge of the loft.

Time dragged on slowly and Ace wondered how long he was to hang like this. The pain in his arms was almost unbearable.

Without warning, a knock sounded at the door of the barn — one, two, three — one — one two. Rafferty opened it and emerged. She was back almost at once.

'Very well, gentlemen. The boss has arrived and we are free to return to London.' She turned to Ace. 'Goodbye, Mr. Lannigan!'

Ace contrived a smile. 'Not goodbye, my dear widder! Let's just say *au revoir*.'

Rafferty blew out the oil lamp, leaving Ace in darkness. They filed out, Rafferty disdaining to answer. As the sound of their car died in the distance, Ace saw a dim shadow enter the barn. The beam of a powerful torch cut through the darkness and focused on Ace. He blinked and tried to pierce the gloom behind it. A hand appeared in front of the torch. It held a revolver. Ace knew this was it; his luck had deserted him completely. He was in a jam from which there was no escape. He knew that that gun was to be his end, his destiny. And with the realisation came the desire to live. He didn't want to die.

Through the open door he could see a patch of summer sky in which the stars were twinkling. He thought of Elsa . . . his work . . . his reputation for being lucky. Well, this was one time his luck was not going to hold. He remembered Mr. King and wondered if that lunk-headed gentleman would ever get his wish and wipe out Ricky's murderer.

'We come to the last mile, eh?' Ace said dryly.

He was shocked to hear a woman's voice reply — a voice distorted with hate and the lust to kill. 'The last mile for you, Lannigan,' she said. 'You might have known that your luck only lasts so long. I think it has run out now!'

'Who are you?' said Ace tautly. 'Since you are to be my murderer — '

'Let us say executioner, Mr. Lannigan.'

'I said murderer — or rather, murderess.'

'Very well; it is of no importance. I admit your right to know, Mr. Lannigan. I am Michael Rafferty's mother.'

Ace Lannigan cursed himself for not thinking of that solution before. Rafferty's wife, and now his mother. No wonder Mrs. Rafferty the younger had taken no offence when he had cracked about the boss taking over Rafferty's business and his woman.

'I was unaware that Rafferty had a mother,' he said.

'Mr. Lannigan, you surprise me. Were you under the impression that he was found on a gooseberry bush?'

Ace glanced once more at the open doorway and the stars. What he would have given for the opportunity to escape — just the slightest chance. But there was no chance, none at all. This was *it*. This was where 'Lucky Lannigan' got the business.

The scent of the fresh hay borne on the night air brought to him that horror of death again. It was not cowardice, for Ace could never have been a coward. It was simply a tearing regret to be leaving the world with so much territory unexplored — so many perilous adventures to be undertaken; so many soft lips and tender eyes to look into. He smiled at himself and his thoughts. Nearly all his life he had courted death — and now that the betrothal was imminent, he shrank from it. He only dimly noted the dark figure that slipped into the barn doorway.

'Life is sweet, is it not?' said the voice of the woman. 'Life was just as sweet, Mr. Lannigan, for the man you sent to the chair. Mike Rafferty loved life!'

'So did the man he murdered!'

'And so it is easily seen by you, Mr. Lannigan! You no doubt wonder why, after having waited for this moment so many long months, I do not fire! The answer is that I want you to realise that of which you are being deprived — life itself. You never could leave well enough alone. Now you must answer for that unfortunate curiosity. Fate has dealt kindly with you, Mr. Lannigan; but though fate may be the ringmaster, destiny is always the owner. With fate you have taken liberties — but you cannot elude destiny!'

Lannigan saw her fingers tighten on the revolver butt and tensed himself. 'Wait!' he said, battling for time. 'Are you going to shoot me without revealing your identity?'

'It is enough for you to know that I am Mike's mother — and as he was my only child, I worshipped him. Our time together was of necessity limited; therefore I detest you for taking him from me.'

Once again those knuckles showed white in glare of the torch; once again Ace smelt death in the muzzle of that black weapon — and once again Mr. King salvaged Ace Lannigan's life.

Joey's movements were fast, and the torch had been knocked from the woman's hand before she realised that she was being attacked; her revolver hand was seized in Joey's own and twisted without mercy. She made no sound, but fought silently tooth and nail, and Joey reeled in momentary panic as her fingernails drew long raking strips of skin from his face, narrowly missing his eye. Much as he regretted it, he was compelled to hit her. Ace, who had been unable to see the struggle, listened anxiously for indications of its progress.

The fallen torch had smashed against some iron spades, and Ace was completely in the dark in more than one way; but a smile was forming on his lips, and his spirits were soaring. It began to appear that destiny was not yet to exact her revenge. He felt fumbling hands at his wrists and heard with relief the well-known bass tone of Mr. King.

'Youse okay, boss?'

'Joey!' Ace grinned. 'Joey, you old son of a gun! How in hell'd you get here?'

'I guess I just followed you, boss!' He took a sharp penknife from his pocket and commenced to saw patiently through the ropes that held Ace. It was accomplished in a second, and Ace fell to the floor, his legs too weak to support him.

'Where's the woman, Joey?'

'I hit de dame, boss,' said Mr. King, as if that were sufficient indication of where she was.

'Good! Let's have a look at her.' Ace struck a match and held it above his head. The boss was gone. Not a trace left. He gazed at Mr. King ruefully. 'I thought you *hit* her, Joey?'

'Sure I did, boss. I didn't like hitting de dame too hard, though. Geeze, de dame mus' be as hard as a baseball bat, Chief. De smack I handed her woulda put any ordinary skoit outa thu woild for at least twenty minutes.'

'You got the revolver?'

'Sure!'

Ace had been massaging his aching legs, but now he stood up with grim determination. 'She can't be far,' he said. 'I didn't hear her come in any car. She just simply arrived. Come on!' They left the barn.

'I was hidin' behind that hedge when she came,' Joey said. 'Only it was too dark to get a load of de dame. From what I hears, though, she comes from up the road here.'

They started along the road as quietly as possible, pausing at intervals to listen. Ace could not help marvelling at his luck as Joey King told him how he had come to follow in the wake of the kidnappers, and of his bumpy journey on the rear of the car. Probably Ace had had his fair share of breaks for the night.

At any rate they found no one, and dawn was breaking before they arrived at the nearest village. Here they were lucky enough to rouse a garage proprietor and requisition a car for their journey home.

It was another Lannigan scoop for the *Gazette*; and Ace, thinking he had had quite sufficient knocks to last for a week or so, accepted an invitation from the Duchess of Deemstown to stay at her country house for a week or so — not because he particularly cared for the company of the dear duchess (far from it), but because it would give him a chance to put in a spot of heavy romance with her charming secretary, Elsa, who was due down in a few days. Meanwhile, Ace found out quite a lot from the garrulous duchess. He learned that in her younger days, she had had a scandalous affair with an Irish music-hall artist, but the matter had been hushed up, and few were in the know. The late duke, her husband, being a mild, somewhat weak man, had forgiven her indiscretion and allowed her to remain as his wife. Gazing at her now, the reporter found it hard to believe. Had Ace been the duke, he would have welcomed any chance to have rid himself of this brightly garbed effusion. Of course, perhaps she had been different then. At present, attired in a flowing purple gown with silver trimmings, she was a picture of horror. Her red, stupid features and her carefully dressed fair hair completed the picture of colourful aristocracy.

She talked to Ace at great length. She talked of her late husband the duke. She touched on the subject of her sponging relatives, her cousins, brothers, sisters, and a few more (the duchess had no children), and she concluded by abusing sweetly her dearest friends. Ace was bored to tears. His polite yawns had no effect upon her. She finally excused herself for a moment or two, saying that she must see about some household details, but adding that she would be back in no time, and had such a lot more to tell him. She took her departure through the door, and Ace, at the risk of being considered terribly, terribly rude, took *his* through the window.

There was a wintry nip in the air that Ace revelled in. He started off at a long swinging walk across the domains of the duchess. The path led past a deep greenish lake to a wood; and Ace, breathing deeply and glad to be alive on this fresh, clean morning, dismissed his irritating problems and concentrated on his enjoyment of the wonders of nature. He had walked for miles when a twinge from his stomach and a glance at his watch told him that if he did not hurry he would be late for lunch. He started to retrace his steps, moving briskly, and soon he was passing the lake he had noticed on his outward journey. It was more luck than anything else.

He had paused to gaze at a swan from the concealment of the trees, when his keen eyes quite plainly saw Mrs. Rafferty the younger!

There was in the centre of the lake a small island and a cluster of trees; and as he watched, the woman vanished into them. Petrified, Ace forgot the time;

forgot his lunch. For long minutes he waited for her to emerge, but she did not.

He found a small boat moored at the edge of the water and, climbing in, he poled it rapidly towards the island. Here he moored it and went carefully into the trees. In the middle of the cluster there was a clearing, and here at some time a small bungalow had been built. It was decrepit from age now, Ace saw. The walls were mildewed and weeds grew in glorious profusion about the veranda.

Quickly he stepped towards it and through the open door — but the bungalow was empty. Ace grunted with chagrin and ran outside. A rapid search served to show that the island was deserted. Probably Rafferty had departed by boat from the opposite side to Ace. A small skiff tied to a post in the bank, opposite the island, pointed to this theory. But what on earth was Rafferty's widow doing here? Had she found out that Ace was staying with the duchess? Was there to be some fresh attempt on his life?

He returned thoughtfully to the bungalow and subjected it to a thorough search.

Nothing seemed to be amiss, but for some reason his eyes riveted on a gigantic wooden wardrobe. It seemed a little incongruous in these surroundings and was firmly bolted to the floorboards. Ace tried the door. It was locked. Without thinking twice, he seized a heavy piece of iron piping and smashed the lock. The wardrobe was entirely devoid of anything; it was an immense size and seemed even larger from the inside.

A careful examination revealed that the bottom of the wardrobe was slightly lower than the level of the floorboards of the bungalow. Ace was intrigued. He spent a long time searching for a possible hidden lever; and finally, giving this up, he inserted the iron bar beneath the flooring of the wardrobe and strained. A semi-rotten board snapped off. Kneeling, Ace applied his eye to the opening. Below was stygian blackness, but he detected a fresh current of air rising from the gap. He conducted a vigorous assault on the remaining boards, and was gratified to see an iron ladder extending downwards. The aperture being large enough, he commenced to descend.

It proved to be a short distance to the bottom of the pit, and groping round in the dimness he found a tunnel running off to the right. He followed this and suddenly realised how Mrs. Rafferty had taken her departure.

The tunnel must run underneath the lake, he reasoned. He followed it slowly and came to an intersection where the tunnel split, one side running to the left and the other straight on. He paused in indecision, and as he did so he became aware of footsteps approaching from the left-hand tunnel.

He pressed close to the wall and held his breath. The footsteps came cautiously nearer, and a bulky figure carrying a torch was visible. It stopped, almost under Ace's nose, and he wound a tight arm about its throat. There was a startled howl . . .

★   ★   ★

Meanwhile, Mr. King, who had not been included in the invitation, was hard at work. By sheer chance he had spotted

Mrs. Rafferty in a London public house!

Joey's brain, not overly strong, was at least strong enough to realise that it might be to his boss's advantage if he tailed her. Struck by a — for him — brilliant idea, he left the bar room and, ambling down the side street, found the open-topped sports car he knew belonged to the gangster's wife. It was untenanted, and after a cautious glance round Joey remedied this by squeezing himself into the rear compartment, crouching on the floor and drawing a large travelling rug about his body. He lost track of time, and was almost on the point of dozing off when he became aware of the jolting rhythm of the car, which was sweeping forward. It was still dark, but Joey dared not risk raising his covering to see where he was. He remained crouched up, suffering agonies of cramp. His power of endurance was stretched to the limit. Once he was startled almost out of his wits when a groping hand reached over into the rear of the car and whipped the travelling rug from him. Mrs. Rafferty was cold. However, she could not permit her eyes to wander from the road, and Joey remained undetected.

It was morning when the car finally halted, but Rafferty did not emerge. She sat on in the front seat smoking cigarette after cigarette, with Joey fervently wishing and hoping that she would not gaze behind her. Eventually he heard the car door open and close.

Somewhat unwisely, he popped his head up and saw the woman leaning against the radiator of the car, trying to gain a little warmth from it. They had parked in a narrow lane, hardly more than a cart track, and about half a mile away a big country house was visible. Rafferty was keeping a steadfast watch on this house, and Joey proceeded to do likewise. He was rewarded by three sudden flashes from one of the windows — flashes caused by a mirror catching the rays of the sun. These were evidently what Rafferty had been waiting for, for without turning she commenced to cross a field and vanished into the woods that surrounded the house. Scarcely pausing to exercise his tortured muscles, Joey followed her.

Mrs. Rafferty was cold and annoyed. It was just like the boss to keep her hanging about waiting for instructions. It was not the first time it had happened. However, the signal had come, and perhaps the boss had been unable conveniently to get away before now. She fought back her irritation and walked swiftly down into the little hollow, hidden by the tangled mass of undergrowth. She peered about her and raised the carpet of matted verdure that covered the entrance to the tunnel.

She had covered half the distance to the island when a sudden whisper stopped her further progress.

'Is that you?' she asked, peering into the gloom.

'Of course it is, you fool!' snapped a woman's harsh voice.

'I waited a long time!' Mrs. Rafferty said plaintively.

'Lannigan is staying at the house,' the other said, ignoring her companion's complaint. 'I shall see if I can manage to get him myself. You must return to London and lie low for a time. Don't come here again until I send for you.'

'Very well — it was just that I wished to see you.'

'Who's that?' breathed the boss suddenly. The two women listened. Along the tunnel, in the direction from which the younger Mrs. Rafferty had come, soft footsteps were audible.

'Quick!' breathed the boss. 'You may have been followed. Go along to the bungalow; you will find a skiff moored at the side of the island. Go back that way. Don't worry about being seen. Everyone is preparing for lunch at the house. Do nothing until you hear from me again. I'll try to finish Lannigan myself!'

The two women parted, the boss retracing steps along the main tunnel and the younger Mrs. Rafferty hurrying to the island. She emerged from the bungalow and came out on the house side. There was no boat moored there save an old punt, and that was on the other side of the lake. She tried the opposite side and found the skiff, then hastily got aboard and paddled rapidly away.

Meanwhile Joey King, following the

tunnel, had arrived at the trapdoor in the wardrobe. Unable to find a way of opening this (to Joey, who was unaware even that it could be opened, it seemed like a dead end), he retraced his steps. Coming up the tunnel, he had thought he had heard voices. He returned silently along the route he had already come, as far as the entrance. Then he turned and commenced again to scour the tunnel. Mrs. Rafferty must be somewhere, he decided. He found his torch and switched it on. He came to the intersection of the tunnel, and was just debating whether he should examine the path he had just found, when a strong vice-like arm wound about his throat. Then he heard a well-known voice say, 'Now, my pippin! Just who are you?'

'Boss! It's me, Joey!' yelled the astonished Mr. King.

'What!' gasped Ace, directing the torch upon its holder. 'How in hell did you get here?'

Joey told him.

'Which window did you say the signal came from?' asked Ace.

Joey scratched his bullet head. 'Geeze! I

don't remember, boss!'

'Anyway, it looks very much as though the boss is in the house,' said Ace. 'If I'm not far out, the Rafferty moll would hardly have made an all-night journey to see anyone other than the boss. What's more, you say you heard voices? Well, I'll give you ten to one that she's *seen* the boss. Stop me if you've heard it, but I rather think that this passage leads to the house itself. Anyhow, the Rafferty widow will be well away by now. I saw her on the island and she must have crossed the other side. Let's try along here!'

They tried the left-hand tunnel, Joey caressing his neck tenderly. They had walked for about ten minutes when they came up against a blank block of wood. The light of the torch revealed that there were two grooves in this. Ace gripped it and pushed with no result. He strained it sideways and it slid slowly aside. Ace stepped out, followed by Joey.

They were in the library. The front of the secret passage was camouflaged by an immense full-length mirror. Ace closed it behind him.

'Remember, Joey,' he said, 'not a word to a soul about this! I'll tell the other guests that you just arrived, and the duchess will be too, *too* delighted to put you up for a few nights. Maybe I'll need you yet!'

'Okay boss!' said Joey.

11

Midnight Merriment

The fun and frolics commenced that very night. Still somewhat exhausted from the events of the past few days, Ace soon took his leave of the company and Elsa. He slept soundly, but his subconscious mind was attuned for any sound that might bode him ill.

He woke to hear a clock chiming one; there was a stillness about the room that seemed unnatural. He saw a dark bulk bending over him and lay quite still. He saw a hand holding a dagger go up for a strike . . .

With a sudden twist and heave, Ace jerked himself from the bed and onto the floor. He was up almost immediately, but the dark intruder was gone in panic, the door slamming faintly.

Ace tore out into the passage, and in his haste blundered against a table, overturning it. The bang of table meeting floor echoed through the gloomy house and Ace cursed roundly. A light had snapped on and doors were opening along the passage.

The duchess came bustling from her room, purple in the face. 'Mr. Lannigan!' she gasped in surprise. 'Did you make that awful noise?'

'I'm afraid I did, Duchess,' Ace said. 'I was attacked in my room by someone with a slight souvenir they meant me to have, in the shape of a dagger.'

The duchess gaped at him unbelievingly. 'In *my* house? Oh, my poor dear Mr. Lannigan, I'm sure you are mistaken!'

The rest of the guests had heard her raucous voice and were gathering about Ace with startled questions.

'I'm afraid not,' said Ace apologetically, but with a touch of acerbity. 'I am not in the habit of seeing things, Duchess!'

The duchess went an even more vivid shade of purple. 'Of course not! Certainly — certainly not!' she said emphatically. 'Please forgive the remark I made, my dear, er, Ace!' She ogled like a coy schoolgirl. 'Yet who could it have been, I wonder?'

Ace gazed at the circle of faces about him. There were quite a few who he was entirely unacquainted with. They all seemed above reproach, except . . .

He motioned to the duchess that she should tell the others to return to bed. They went off muttering, some visibly agitated by the idea that there was a prowler in the house.

'Probably some wicked burglar from outside,' suggested the Duchess brightly.

Ace smiled. 'Who was the short stout lady?' he asked. 'The one in the pink negligee? I don't think I have met her before.'

'She was never introduced to you, Mr. Lannigan. Of course, you know she may have reason to be afraid of you reporters.'

'How's that?'

'Well, I don't know her, not really, but she has come with the Bagley-Joneses; a friend of theirs. They met her while they were in Miami. I think perhaps she doesn't want to be introduced to you because you might remember too much about her — her past. I believe she wasn't a very moral person,' said the Duchess primly. 'But, of course, we broadminded people are above such trivial matters — we are of the world!' And she ogled in a way that made Ace feel quite sick.

'But why should she imagine that I might recall her murky past?' he asked.

'Well, I understand she was rather well known in Miami society — in fact, some of the things Mrs. Bagley-Jones told me — well . . . ' The duchess paused meaningfully. 'Perhaps you *do* remember some little episode — ?'

'Not a thing,' Ace told her. 'What is the woman's name?'

The duchess seemed a little disappointed in not getting any dirt about the American woman. Ace's questions had convinced her that he knew something. 'The name is, er, Royce. Mrs. Edith Royce. Of course, her husband is alive, but she hardly ever seems to be with him. They say in London, Ace, that while she has been here — '

'Good night, Duchess!' said Ace quite rudely. 'Sleep tight!'

The duchess seemed as if she would have hysterics for a second. Then, bidding him an injured 'Good night', she took her departure.

Joey King had not left with the rest of the guests, and he now announced his intention of sleeping in Ace's room. Smiling, Ace gave him the okay. It was easy to see that if there was going to be any death, Joey wanted to be in on it.

But the remainder of the night passed calmly enough; and in spite of the attempt on his life, Ace did full justice to his need to rest. As for that impeccable guardian of the small hours, Mr. Joey King, it would have taken a small earthquake to have awakened him.

It had been arranged between Ace and Elsa that they would go riding on the morrow; and when Joey suggested that he should come along, Ace had acquiesced. Well aware that Mr. King could not ride, Ace thought that it would be incredibly funny to see him on horseback. Mr. King, in his determination to protect Ace, for whom he had conceived a deep and touching affection, saw the riding part of it as just an elementary object; an obstacle to be easily overcome by such a vast intelligence as his own.

'Have you ever done equestrian work?' asked Ace as they assembled the following morning.

'Naw; I guess I ain't done no work at all, boss, an' I never did care much for them fancy-sounding jobs.'

Which remark caused Elsa to gurgle convulsively.

'I mean, have you ever ridden a horse?'

'Geeze,' said Joey in wonder, 'is dat what youse meant, boss?'

'That's it. Well, have you?'

'Guess not, boss. I once had a ride on an elefunt down at Coney Island, though. Geeze, dat was sure some thrill!' Joey's eyes glistened at the memory.

They arrived at the stables, Ace giving Joey last-minute directions that might as well have been addressed to the wall for all Mr. King grasped of them.

'To mount,' said Ace, 'place one foot in the stirrup — '

'Holy Mike! An' I got my noo dogs on — '

'What of it?' The stirrup won't harm them.'

'Stirrup? I tought youse said syrup, boss. I likes dat — with flapjacks!'

'No doubt. Once on, just keep the rein off the horse's neck — '

'It ain't rainin', boss. Besides — '

'The rein, you dope!' said Ace. 'The *rein* you guide the nag with. Keep it tight!'

'Oh! Sure, I'll do dat.'

'Then the nag won't bolt with you. When you want the horse to canter — '

'Now dat guy's a vurry fine singer,' admitted Joey irrelevantly. 'I seen de dope in de *Roman Scandals*. Geeze, boss, de boids what was in that picture!'

'Not Eddie Cantor,' hissed Ace. 'Get on the horse.'

Joey eyed the horse with misgiving. 'Geeze, de nag seems a bit taller dan de Empire State Building from where I'm standing!'

The groom grinned and brought the horse to Joey's side. It was a supreme animal, graceful of line and possessing a fiery eye and a noble mane. The fiery eye was what worried Mr. King. He placed a cautious foot in the stirrup as instructed. The horse stood stock-still. The groom seized Joey's other leg and gave him a boost. He landed with a thump in the saddle. The horse turned and regarded him with a suspicious eye.

His hat lay some three yards away, whence it had rolled. The groom picked it up and handed it to him. Joey released his hold on the mane to pop it on his dome-like skull. The horse moved. Ace and Elsa picked Mr. King up and hauled him away from the horse, which seemed bent on eating his long-suffering bowler.

'Try again!' said Ace.

Joey looked uncomfortable. 'Well, I don't tink nothink'll happen to youse, on second thoughts, boss. If it's all de same by you, I guess I'll take a walk,' he said tentatively. 'My arches has been falling somethin' shockin' lately, an' a walk's de only ting — '

'Okay, Joey!' said Ace with a grin. 'I guess we'll be able to struggle through on our own.'

He and Elsa mounted their horses and

trotted away out of the stable yard. Mr. King became aware of the stable lad grinning at him, and hastily removed himself and his bruised posterior to the sanctity of the summer house.

The two equestrians rode without speaking for some miles. Then, finding themselves in a tiny valley, they dismounted and opened the sandwiches Elsa had brought along.

'Ace, aren't you ever going to give up all this trouble-hunting?' she asked him as he munched his sandwich.

Ace stopped munching and looked her in the eyes. 'I guess not, kid,' he said seriously. 'You see, I'm the guy who wasn't cut out to be tied down. I'm the chump who has to play with the breaks. That's me. Put a halter on me and I'd be a dead duck. I like you plenty, Elsa — but that's as far as I'm going to go.'

She was silent, looking at the surrounding hills glowing with late daffodils. 'Why, Ace?' she asked. 'Why couldn't you settle down? Surely if you just gave it a trial — '

Ace shook his head. 'That wouldn't be playing it square. Don't worry, Elsa — I won't be forgetting you for a long time. But it wouldn't be right to settle down, then suddenly get the urge — '

'But if you had the right woman — and — and you wanted to go looking for trouble, I — I guess — if she was the right woman, she'd be glad to come along.'

Ace shook his head again. 'Wouldn't be right, kid.' He bent and kissed her. 'You're a swell kid, Elsa, and don't think I'm too thick to know what you're getting at! Maybe at present I'd like it that way myself, but I know it wouldn't last. At the best of times I'm a queer cuss!'

They let the matter drop there. There was nothing more to say.

The bullet came whistling from out of the hills and slapped into the tree trunk by Ace's head. In no time he had scooped himself and Elsa into the trees behind them. Elsa was alarmed and scared.

'High-powered rifle,' commented Ace, scanning the hills keenly.

'Could it be someone out hunting?' asked Elsa, getting her nerves under control.

'Yeah — man-hunting,' said Ace

sarcastically. Keeping the two horses between himself and the opposite slope, he edged to their tethering ropes and led them briskly into the shelter of the trees. 'Guess we won't hang about here any longer,' he said. 'Best be getting back to the house.'

They led the horses through the trees and, mounting, started for home at a brisk pace. Mr. King met them as they were entering the stable yard.

'Hi, boss!' he beamed. 'I told youse nothin'd happen today, huh?'

'That's right,' said Ace. 'But your optimistic prophecies were unduly shattered, you lunk!' And, leaving Joey to figure that one out, they entered the house.

In the library they came unexpectedly across Mrs. Edith Royce and the duchess. They flushed guiltily as Ace entered and began to prattle of this and that. Ace, however, had caught a little of their previous conversation, and he fixed the duchess with a glittering eye.

'Did I hear you ladies suggest that I was given to imagining things?' he asked.

'No, dear me, no!' blabbered the

embarrassed duchess.

Ace ignored Elsa's reproachful looks. 'Because if so, perhaps you will tell me I imagined this!' He crossed to the mirror and heaved it rapidly to one side, intending to watch their reactions. Only there was a slight hitch. The mirror did not budge. Ace desisted as he realised it must be locked from the inside, and the two ladies glanced at each other knowingly.

'Er — what was it, Mr. Lannigan?' said the duchess.

Ace grinned. 'Oh, it wasn't anything. Except — is there a hidden tunnel behind that mirror, Duchess?'

The duchess seemed surprised. 'As a matter of fact, there is! My, though, how clever of you to suspect it!'

'Where do you keep the key?'

'There is no key, Mr. Lannigan. The control for opening that passage has not worked in months — years — centuries.'

'That's quite a long time, Duchess. Where are the controls?'

'To be truthful, I don't quite know, but there is an old plan of the house in one of

those volumes of Dickens's works. Here!'
She crossed to a shelf and extracted a
dusty volume. 'Why, it's gone!' she
gasped. 'Now who on earth would want
that?'

'I have no idea, Duchess,' replied Ace.
'But I rather think — at least, it would
hardly surprise me — if it were not the
gang who kidnapped you before. I fancy
they are back on the scent!'

With which remark he left the room
for the garages in order to inspect the
duchess's fleet of cars, and had the
somewhat dubious satisfaction of hearing
the duchess have a fit of hysterics as he
went.

Elsa came after him. 'Why on earth did
you frighten the old dear?' she asked
indignantly. 'It was an awful thing to do!'

'Come off it, Elsa,' he said. 'You know
as well as I do that those hysterics are
an act. Besides, I wanted to note Mrs.
Royce's reaction to what I said.'

'And did you?'

'I did not. Either she has no connection
with all this, or else she has remarkable
control of her features.'

They spent the rest of the day testing the various cars, and a few subtle questions elicited from the chauffeur the information that Mrs. Royce had had a car out about an hour earlier.

'Which once again,' mused Ace, fishing a high-powered rifle from the seat of the car he was examining, 'puts the onus on Mrs. Royce.' He turned to the chauffeur. 'Was this the car she took?'

'I'm afraid I really couldn't tell you, sir. You see, so many look alike, and I am continually shunting them in and out of line.'

'Anyone else take a car?'

'Not to my knowledge. Of course, I went to the village shortly after Mrs. Royce left. In fact, it was while on my way there that I observed her drive out. I was walking at the time; I get *that* sick of cars!' he burst out, suddenly becoming human.

Ace pressed a tip on him and they proceeded on their way.

12

The End of the House Party

Ace obtained no more clues during his stay at the house of the Duchess of Deemstown. The activities of the gang seemed to have ceased with the failure to kill Ace in those two attempts. The house party broke up one week later, and Ace took his adieus of the duchess, who was devastated that he was going, but who said that if he must — and she assumed he must — would he please take it for granted that the absolute freedom of the house was his any time he cared to utilise it. Ace assured her he would, and said his goodbyes to Elsa, who was remaining at the house with the duchess in order to attend to the details of closing it down for the winter and dispatching the servants to the duchess's town house; a fact the duchess had overlooked when she had gushingly extended to Ace the freedom of the house.

He and Joey King arrived back at the flat just after teatime that evening, and Ace wondered idly what he might do now that Elsa was not in town, and now that the gang had vanished. He threw on his coat and hat, glanced at the already snoring Joey, and swept out into the night. His trail led him to the hotel at which he had learned Mrs. E. Royce was residing. He did not bother to send up his card, but dropped in just as she was taking tea.

'Sit down, Mr. Lannigan,' she said, betraying no surprise. 'Will you take tea?'

'Please,' said Ace. He watched her closely as she poured it out.

'Now what did you want?' she asked him.

'One or two things,' he told her, 'assuming that *you are Mike Rafferty's mother!*'

If he had expected to take her by storm, he was unsuccessful. 'Mr. Lannigan!' she said. 'That's hardly a compliment, is it?'

'It's hardly meant as one,' he told her grimly. 'But if such is not the case, why did you try to avoid me when I first arrived at the house party?'

She gave him a watery smile. 'I should have thought the duchess told you. The remarkable quality about that charming soul is her tongue — like a babbling brook, it goes on forever.'

'The duchess told me a thing or two,' acknowledged Ace. 'She hinted that you had a skeleton in the family closet.'

'I have. A rather grim one, Mr. Lannigan. I was associated with Mike Rafferty, but not as a mother — oh dear, no! To be quite candid — and if I have your word of honour, Mr. Lannigan, that you will not divulge what I tell you — '

Ace nodded. 'You have.'

'I was Mr. Rafferty's mistress, then. There! Now you have the shameful secret.'

'Impossible,' said Ace. 'A woman as old — I beg your pardon; I should have said that the difference in age — '

'The difference in age was immaterial. I was Rafferty's mistress until he had had time to collect a nice bunch of rather warmish middle-aged love letters. Then I ceased to be his mistress and became his victim! I paid through the nose to prevent my husband from seeing those letters. It was a business with him. Indeed, I was deeply grateful when you sent him to the chair, Lannigan. More tea?'

'No, thanks. Then if you were his mistress, surely you must know who his mother was?'

'Not at all. He never admitted me into his confidence to that extent.'

'Did he know himself?'

'I am sure he did! No, I am not concealing anything, for it would not harm me to tell you if I knew. The truth is that I do not know.'

Ace picked up his hat and turned to the door.

'I can tell you one thing, though.'

He stopped and turned. 'Which is?'

'Mike Rafferty was a bastard,' she said sweetly.

'You're telling me,' said Ace. 'Some folks have better names for him than that!'

She smiled again. 'I am not using the term as an epithet. I mean that Mike Rafferty was illegitimate. He never knew his father.'

Ace went out with his head buzzing. So

this was the reason for all the secrecy about Rafferty's parentage. Still, it brought him no nearer to finding the mother.

He returned somewhat disconsolately to his flat, where he found Joey still asleep. He sat down to think it all out. Of course, this Royce woman might be stringing him along, but he hardly thought so. Her tone had been very sincere throughout their chat. The more Ace thought about it, the more his head whirled. He drank whisky copiously and smoked interminably. Everyone bar Mrs. Royce had been a well-noted member of society at that house party. Could he have been mistaken about the boss being there?

The heavy atmosphere took effect and he slept.

The following morning he phoned Elsa and obtained the names and titles of the guests who had attended the duchess's house party. This done, he went along to the nearest reference library and studied *Who's Who* and *Burke's Peerage*. Everyone at that house party seemed to have been above reproach — excluding Mrs. Edith Royce.

With an exasperated snort, he slammed the books closed, earning a reproving glare from the librarian. He wandered out into the busy streets and walked aimlessly through Brixton to Kennington, past the Oval and on. He took the subway and alighted at St. John's Wood. Past Lord's and Elm Tree Road he walked, travelling at random, with no set purpose. The case had him baffled. Obviously the boss was someone with whom he had come into contact at the house party — someone out of the twenty people he had met. Ten of these were male, so they were eliminated. The women had been, as he recalled:

Elsa Daly.

The duchess.

The Countess of Goddam (this was a name of his own coining).

The Right Honourable Celia Duggleston (from the way she had shamelessly chased Ace, she could have been neither right nor honourable).

Mrs. G. Oojah (the names, were, of course, incorrect, but Ace remembered the faces and personalities of those he was dealing with perfectly).

The Thingumabob of Where's-it (he'd forgotten her title entirely).

The Doodad of Devon.

Maisie Audrey Phipps, MP.

Princess Doran of Kotania and her maidservant.

Of these he could eliminate Elsa, the duchess, the princess, the maid, the MP., the countess and Celia Duggleston; and surely the Doodad, the Thingumabob, and Mrs. Oojah were above suspicion. Which merely brought him back to Mrs. Royce.

Irritably he brushed the problem from his mind. Since the boss was so keen on getting him, she would most likely try again. Ace made a mental note to keep his eyes open. He had wandered far during this soliloquy and found himself in the portion of Limehouse that had witnessed his last meeting, with Mrs. Rafferty. Yes — there was the little entry up which he had ventured; there the door he had unwittingly gone through, and —

The door in question opened and a man emerged. Ace dashed across the road and secured a grip on his shoulder. 'Remember me, pal?' he murmured softly.

The Cockney jumped. 'Oo' the 'ell are you, mite?'

'You know, brother, you know. Surely you remember slugging me one night in the not-so-distant past. Of course you do.'

The man, seeing that prevarication would be useless, nodded. 'Yus, oi remember! What of it?'

Ace raised his eyebrows. 'Don't you know that you were an accessory to murder — before the fact, what's more?'

'Blimey! They never told me that. They just said as 'ow they wanted you out o' the wye fer a bit!'

'We'll see if the judge'll believe that.'

''Ere, 'old on. You ain't got no proof as 'ow oi 'it yer!'

'Only that of my assistant, who saw you help to carry me to the car.'

'Blimey!'

'Of course, if you can help me to get in touch with Mrs. Rafferty — '

'She's in there now!' He jerked his thumb towards the door from which he had just emerged.

'In that case perhaps you can let me in?' The man stared at him. 'Or shall I call the cops?'

'Yer wanter go in there, after wat 'appened last toime?'

'That's about it.'

'Yer barmy! Orlright, come along wiv me.' He opened the door for Ace and stood aside.

'You first, pal,' said Ace politely.

The man led the way, and they proceeded along the passage and into the room in which Ace had been sandbagged. This was empty, and the guide crossed it and went through the opposite door.

They were in an opium den. It was devoid of windows, and heavily hung with silken drapes. In one corner a wizened Chinaman sat by a smouldering brazier, and by him a large collection of long-stemmed pipes was visible. About the room, lying with enigmatic smiles, some sprawled unnaturally, some perfectly relaxed, lay a number of Chinese of all ages. One of them was moaning softly, his black skull cap clutched in a twisted hand. Ace cast a glance of revulsion at an unkempt white man who lay drugged among the Chinese. The wizened man by the brazier did not glance up as they passed through. Behind the dope chamber were a number of cubicles with silken curtains drawn across the fronts. From one of these came a woman's laugh and a man's coarse chuckle. Ace had seen many of these dope parlours in the Sates, and they always left him feeling contemptuous of his fellow men. This one was no exception. He shuddered involuntarily and pressed on after his guide. The Cockney had paused at a heavy oak door, and now he knocked on it tentatively.

A woman's voice bade him enter.

'There you are, mate,' he whispered to Ace. 'She's in there. For Gawd's sake, don't tell 'er 'oo brought you in!' And he retreated hastily the way they had come.

Ace jauntily entered the room and saw the younger Mrs. Rafferty lying upon a low divan, surrounded by silken cushions. She was attired in an almost transparent negligee and very little else. Her cornflower hair spread in fair cascades upon the black silk of the divan, and a cigarette rested between her red lips. Her cloudy blue eyes were far away, gazing into the distance, and Ace realised with a sudden shock that the cigarette she was smoking was doped — her face bore the dreamy, enigmatic look of a dope smoker. She was not fully under its influence, and turned and regarded him vaguely, her negligee falling open, revealing an ivory white limb.

'I think I know you,' she said languidly. 'Have you been here before?'

She was too far gone to be able to place him clearly. He nodded.

'Will you have a cigarette?' She extended a plain paper packet towards him. He accepted one, slid it in his pocket and replaced it quickly with one of his own, for he was a little wary yet.

Her next words showed that he had been wise. She lit it for him. 'Marijuana!' she told him vaguely. 'They're much better when taken in company with a man.'

He knew that; knew all about the wretched sexual depravities that could arise from the smoking of marijuana. He was glad she had not noticed him changing the cigarette, and decided to play along with her. Maybe he would get something out of her while she was like this.

She extended a slim hand and drew him down beside her. Looking at her, he wondered again how she had come to fall in love with Rafferty. Now there was none of the habitual harshness in her glance or her voice. The drug had reached the point where its victim was reduced to maudlin sentimentality. For a moment he experienced a twinge of pity for the beautiful widow; then his heart hardened as he recalled the torture he had been through, instigated by that languid mind which sat beside him encased in that body of deceptive loveliness; recalled those pale, slender hands which rested now in his own, tearing the bandages from his wounded head.

Rafferty had moved closer. The scent she used, the warmth of her supple body, and her fair hair on his shoulder almost lost the day for Ace.

He questioned her; dragged her dream-ridden, wandering mind back from the limbo of fantasy; dragged from her the confirmation that her late husband had been illegitimate. He had been accustomed to seeing his mother once a year in Honolulu. Apparently he had been fond of her, yes. No, she couldn't remember his mother's name. Her drugged mind could not single out the information. Yes, his mother had been English.

She continued smoking as Ace questioned her, and the fumes in the room began to erode the tight grip he had upon himself. As soon as he realised he would not obtain any more information from her, he left the room. She lay on the divan, so far gone that she made no move to prevent his departure.

He passed through the dope parlour and out into the clean air. He walked home, and once there tumbled fully clad onto the bed and slept. The telephone rang repeatedly, but he could not answer it. Joey King rolled in, and after his first surprise, partially undressed him and put him between the sheets. Then he, too, fell asleep on the settee, and the silence was only broken by his snores and the ringing of the telephone.

At the other end of the line, Michael Woodson, Ace's editor, cursed fluently. He had been ringing Ace's flat for a full hour and had received the same answer each time — 'Sorry, your number does not reply.'

He fumed and raged. If Lannigan thought he could do this sort of thing — Ace had not been into the office or seen his editor since his return from the duchess — he was mistaken. There would have to be a change, decided Woodson, rattling his phone again.

Still no answer. He seized his hat and coat and strode from the office.

13

Arrest Ace Lannigan!

Michael Woodson arrived at the flat and hammered at the door for several minutes before he aroused Ace sufficiently for him to stagger out of the bed and answer. Woodson glared at the half-dressed figure and pushed into the flat.

'What the dickens do you mean by not reporting to the office? Don't you know that we might have had some important information for you? We couldn't get you on the phone — why the devil don't you let us know where we can get in touch with you if we need to? I've been ringing your damned number for a hundred years, and all I get is 'No answer'!' He paused to gather breath.

Ace blinked blearily. 'Hello, Chief.'

'Hello be damned! Don't you know that the police are after you? I don't know what you're going to do, but take my word you'd better get moving if you don't want to be put away for a spell. I dare say they'll be calling to collect you any moment now. Then who'll take the case on?'

Ace was fully alert. 'The police? What the devil do they want me for?'

'It appears that a fool of a constable whom you once knocked out in Limehouse recognised you from a photograph this morning and reported the matter to the Yard. Inspector Briggs rang up to tell me that you wouldn't have a chance to finish the case, or at least you'd have to let it drop, as they had no alternative but to lock you up for assaulting a police officer in the execution of his duty. Mark my words, Ace, they will put you away for a while. It's a serious thing you did.'

'Suffering Mike!' groaned Ace. 'I forgot all about that!'

'I think Briggs's idea in phoning me and tipping me off was so that you could make a break for it, if you wanted; but believe me, you'll have to get going if you are going!'

Ace had collected a suitcase and was

hastily packing it with a few odds and ends. Mr. King awakened and was blinking in puzzlement at the two men.

'Quick, Ace!' cried Woodson. 'Slide out the back way. There's a police car outside the door!'

'Let you know where I get to!' panted Ace, and he shot through the door and down the back stairs. As he did so, Inspector Briggs, accompanied by a plainclothes man, hammered at the front door. Michael Woodson admitted them.

'Where's Lannigan?' demanded Briggs.

The editor looked puzzled. 'Lannigan? Hmm! Haven't seen Lannigan for quite a while, now you mention it. Let me see — you wanted him for something or other, didn't you?'

'Assault!' said Briggs briefly. His gaze fell on the hastily opened drawers and disarranged clothing scattered when Ace had packed his case. 'Been packing?'

'Just sorting a few things out for a rummage sale,' yawned Woodson.

'I see,' Briggs replied, and Woodson was nearly certain that the detective-inspector winked at him.

Meanwhile, Ace was hitting the trail and hitting it fast. He had been fortunate in flagging a taxi to the local bus station, where he had taken a bus out of town. He arrived somewhat weary at a small village and made his way to the local inn. It was about eight o'clock, and he ordered a Scotch and sat deliberating on his next move.

And at the flat in London, Joey King was just answering the phone.

'Is that Joey?' panted a woman's voice. 'Will you get Ace for me? Hurry, please; this is Elsa.'

Joey could tell by the strained and almost whispered words that she was in some kind of trouble. 'Ace ain't here. Can I do anythin', lady?' he asked.

'Get in touch with him as soon as possible,' the woman panted. 'Tell him that I know who the boss — '

Suddenly there was silence at the other end of the line. For a second Joey listened. 'Hello?' he said. He heard the receiver replaced.

He dialed enquiries and asked them to trace the call. He fumed impatiently while they did so; then after an agonising lapse of five minutes, they came through again: 'The call came from the Towers, the residence of the Duchess of Deemstown.'

Joey thanked them, grabbed his hat, stuck it on and tore off to the nearest hire garage. He hired a powerful car and started along the almost straight road to Deemstown.

At the same moment, Mrs. Rafferty was receiving a call. 'Come down here at once. There is going to be a showdown. The woman found out and phoned Lannigan. I stopped her before she could reveal my identity, but if I know Lannigan he'll be down here in next to no time. This will be our last chance to finish him off, I think. He won't bring the police — he always works alone. I have absolute control of the house here. All the servants were sent up to London — in fact everything is staged for the complete elimination of Mr. Ace Lannigan.' She rang off, and the younger Mrs. Rafferty shook her dope-drowsy head and went for her car.

At the same moment, Ace had decided

to make his way to the country house of the duchess. He was nowhere near Deemstown, but, with the help of the landlord, who introduced him to a patron who owned a garage, he eventually managed to hire a car.

Once in it, he trod on the gas . . .

So did Joey King . . .

So did the widow . . .

Humming through the night, the three cars converged rapidly on the Towers — and the solution of the mystery . . .

Joey King, disobeying all known traffic rules, arrived first. The house was in darkness and silence and he made his entry through a ground-floor window.

Scarcely was he inside than Mrs. Rafferty arrived, leaving her car a good distance from the house. She entered by the back door, which had been left open for the purpose. She came face to face with Joey King in the hall. She was using a torch, and therefore Joey was at a disadvantage. She shot him down calmly. He fell without a groan — King was out of play.

And Ace, who had witnessed the little

drama — he had entered by the same back door as Mrs. Rafferty, practically on her heels — fired at the direction of the torch, but he was too late to save King. He had the grim satisfaction of knowing that Mrs. Rafferty would never shoot again — she had followed her husband to hell with a bullet in the heart.

Ace, without compunction, wrenched the torch from the woman's clenched hand. Joey King was lying on his back, his breath rasping from his lungs, his eyes closed. As Ace bent over him, they flickered open and he tried to smile.

'Where'd she get you, Joey?' asked Ace.

'In de stummick, boss! Geeze, I guess I stopped a load dat time!' His head dropped back limply, and Ace stood up with a peculiar sensation in his breast. Poor old Joey! It looked as though he wasn't going to get Ricky's killer after all. He had lost consciousness through the pain, and Ace paused, uncertain of his next move.

Suddenly Joey tore himself back from the blackness of senselessness and spoke in a hoarse, gasping whisper: 'De dame — Elsa, boss — she phoned de flat. Said

she knew who de boss was. Sumthin'
happened to her . . . ' His voice trailed
away again as he went under.

Ace whistled. So that was why Joey had
come down here. Then, Elsa . . . ? He
turned and sprinted up the stairs to the
room that had been hers and flung open
the door. The beam from Mrs. Rafferty's
torch cut across to the bed.

Elsa was there, all right. She was bound
and gagged, and her eyes were dazzled in
the torch light. Ace crossed the room and
bent over her, fumbling with the ropes
that bound her, and then — the lights
flashed on!

'Don't move, Lannigan!' said a woman's voice — that of the boss. But Ace did
move, and quickly. He gauged the
position of the speaker and whirled
round, his revolver in his hand. A bullet
tore into his gun hand; his revolver spun
across the room, and he hugged the
smashed hand beneath his armpit. The
Duchess of Deemstown smiled at him
grimly from behind the revolver she held.

'I think you have waited a long time for
this meeting, Ace?'

'I think I have!' Ace betrayed no surprise, but he felt it. He had had his suspicions regarding the woman, but now that they had been proved he was inwardly amazed.

'The end of the trail, my dear, dear Mr. Lannigan,' mocked the duchess; then, her tone changing: 'What were the shots I heard below?'

'I eliminated Mrs. Rafferty,' said Ace with a smile, refusing to show his perturbation.

'That is as well,' said the duchess. 'I should have had to do so myself after I had eliminated you and the charming Elsa. It was a pity she discovered my secret! She found some letters Michael had written to me once, and I was forced to give her a gentle tap when she tried to phone you. A pity, because I had left her my entire estate in my will, and I rather liked her — she took the place of Mike, you see. Now, of course, I can hardly let her live.'

'Mike Rafferty was your son?'

'Michael Rafferty was my illegitimate son, Mr. Lannigan. Quite a furore it caused in my family. His father was an

Irish music-hall comedian. Poor dear O'Rory! He has been dead twenty years now. My father paid him hush money and my baby was taken from me when it was born and sent away to America, left in the care of a Brooklyn couple. I didn't mind much at the time; but later, when I had discovered that my husband the duke, also dead, could not give me a baby — he was very old, you know — I began to think of my one child in America. It would merely be a waste of time to tell you how I contrived to get in touch with him, how we met at Honolulu each year and how we came to feel that love for each other — motherhood is a strange thing, Mr. Lannigan — and how, when you sent poor Michael to the chair, I swore to kill you sooner or later. Of course there were snags, but fortunately they have been overcome.'

'So you arranged to be kidnapped by your own gang as a blind — they didn't even know themselves that you are the boss?'

'That's right, Mr. Lannigan! Rather an old trick, but effective, don't you think? I knew quite a lot about your movements — it was useful having a secretary who was in love with you. She told me quite unknowingly everything you were doing.' She glanced at the bound woman. 'I'm sorry I shall have to do this to you, my dear, believe me. I'm afraid there is no help for it, though.'

Looking into her cold eyes, Ace knew there wasn't. A pity, for there were still a lot of things in the world he would have liked to have done.

'And now, Mr. Lannigan, you may take the gag from your sweetheart's lips and say goodbye. I take it you wish to do so?'

Ace nodded. He bent and removed Elsa's gag, thinking hard. One way or another he would get his — he knew that! But if he could get at the duchess, even if he died in the attempt, he could finish her off and perhaps save Elsa. He bent and kissed her.

'The end of the game, old thing,' he muttered. 'Goodbye, Elsa.'

She held the tears back bravely. 'Goodbye — Ace!'

He turned, preparing to spring — then

paused and held himself rigid. The duchess was talking again, but Ace did not hear her. From the corner of his eye he could see the door behind her opening slowly. A grim, contorted face appeared round the edge of the door. A bowler hat surmounted it.

Joey King!

The duchess, sensing trouble, did not turn her back on Ace, but moved rapidly across the floor so that she commanded a view of the entire room. She saw Mr. King — holding his stomach, a dark red stain spreading over his fingers — advancing upon her. She fired.

Joey jerked upright, but kept on. She fired again wildly — once — twice . . .

Then Joey King was upon her, the light in his eyes savage, avenging. Her revolver hand was knocked aside. His massive hands sought her throat, fingernails clawing into the plump flesh. She scrabbled frantically at his fingers, thin shrieks issuing from her bloodless lips. Her eyes began to protrude, and her tongue. She fought for air.

And Joey, feeling his strength failing, blood spurting from his tortured body, picked her up bodily and smashed her head against the wall.

'Dat for Ricky, sister!' he said hoarsely.

Ace picked him up from the lacerated thing which had been Rafferty's old lady. He was dead — as dead as the duchess.

Ace swallowed a lump in his throat and laid Mr. King on a couch, covering his bleeding frame with an eiderdown. He turned to comfort Elsa as the horrified woman subsided into sobs.

★   ★   ★

It was twilight, and stars were beginning to twinkle in the deep purple of the sky. The rose garden at the Towers was filled with the fragrance of late roses and rusty brown leaves. Ace and Elsa were walking along the path towards the summer house. Ace drew her to a swinging seat. There was a mute appeal in Elsa's eyes. In Ace's there was regret. Regret that the adventure had ended. Regret that Mr. King had proved the saying that 'all flesh is as grass'. Regret that he must leave Elsa.

The matter of the assaulted constable had been pardoned by a grateful country. England was free of the menace. And with a dawning fear and helplessness, Elsa was realising that Ace was going.

He was trying to explain. 'That's the way it is, honey. I'd be a fool to say that I don't just about worship you. That can't count, kid. I can't let it! I'm not going to repeat that line about it not being fair for me to marry you. I just don't happen to be the type to get hitched. I leave for America tomorrow.'

Her heart aching, Elsa raised her head. 'But Ace, you may — may — '

'Get bumped off? Maybe. But I won't be operating in the old quarters. The *Recorder*, my old paper, have an assignment for me in South America. It's a great break. There's a revolution brewing there in one of the minor states, and I'm covering it. Maybe someday I'll be back — but don't wait, kid.' He bent and pressed a light kiss on her lips, gave a short laugh and walked through the gate onto the road.

'Ace! Won't you stay the night?' She

tried to take it bravely, as she knew he expected her to.

'Sorry. Guess there's a train runnin' to London. It'd be better if you don't see me off tomorrow.' His voice was suddenly soft, and he held her eyes. 'I'm sorry, kid, but I must play with the breaks. You know, that's the way it goes. Goodbye, Elsa!'

She watched his tall figure swing down the road into the gathering shadows; saw him turn once and sweep off his battered trilby with a bandaged hand. Then he was gone, and in a nearby tree a nightingale burst into song.

Epilogue

The *Gargantuan* docked at two o'clock. From it stepped a tall man wearing a battered trilby. It was canted at an impossible angle on the back of his fair hair. He passed through customs and made his way to the exit. As he emerged, a large closed car got underway and tore past at a great speed. Ace saw it and went flat. The veteran reporter and the young man with him hurled themselves down to the ground at the same time. A burst of machine-gun fire raked the walls of the landing stage, and the car roared on round the corner. The fair-haired man picked himself up and beckoned to an astonished taxi driver.

'Drive me to the *Recorder* offices, Bud; then wait to take me to the nearest airport running a South American line. Step on it!' The taxi whirled away.

The veteran reporter with the youth by his side pushed his way through to a phone booth and inserted his nickel, then dialed a number.

'Yeah, this is Floyd — covering the waterfront. Now get this. Ace Lannigan came back today. Yep, the mobs musta known about it. They tried to give him a little present of welcome as he left the stage. Yeah, they missed him. Lucky as usual.'

The youth listened to him giving the story and waited for him to replace the receiver. 'Gee! That Ace Lannigan certainly takes the chances,' he said.

'Yeah. The guy's luck can't hold forever, though,' said the man with him. 'Wonder what he's going to cover in South America?'

As Ace boarded the great airliner for Latin America, far away in England a woman sat in a rose garden. The duchess had left her the entire estate, but there was still something missing. Elsa was a very lonely woman. She missed that careless, reckless, laughing cavalier — she missed Ace. There was a large moon shining upon her; stars were twinkling; a nightingale was trilling a plaintive melody. It was a night designed and produced for lovers.

She was alone, save for the ghost of a mocking smile; a bantering voice; a battered trilby and a mop of fair, wavy hair. Alone, except for the ghost of Ace Lannigan; and she realised with a horrible certainty that he had gone forever — that no other could ever take his place.

She heard his soft voice again — ghostly, unreal, a figment of her wretched misery: 'Sorry, kid. That's the way it goes. Guess I just ain't the type to get hitched. Sorry, kid. Play with the breaks. Be a fool to say I don't love you. That's the way it goes. Sorry, kid. Sorry, kid . . . Sorry . . . Sorry . . . ' The rustling trees whispered it; the soft breeze sighed it; the nightingale trilled it — 'Sorry, kid!'

She seemed to see a tall, lithe figure striding along the road towards her. She sprang up with a glad cry, but it was nothing — a phantasm of her broken heart. She sank onto the garden seat, and the moon and stars blurred as a mist crept across her eyes. Tears flowed and eased her unhappiness. And the trees whispered — 'Sorry, kid.'